TONY BRADMAN has written many books for children
of all ages, and has been published all over the world.
He has also edited a large number of highly successful
anthologies of short stories and poems, including *Skin Deep*,
a collection of stories about racism, and *Give Me Shelter*,
stories about children who seek asylum.
Tony has three grown-up children and two grandchildren
and lives in London.

For Lily and Oscar – the future belongs to them!
T.B.

First published in Great Britain in 2009 and in the USA in 2010 by
Frances Lincoln Children's Books, 4 Torriano Mews,
Torriano Avenue, London NW5 2RZ
www.franceslincoln.com

First paperback published in Great Britain and in the USA in 2012

A catalogue record for this book is available from the British Library.

ISBN 978-1-84507-944-4

Set in Sabon LT

Printed and bound by CPI Group (UK) Ltd, Croydon, CR0 4YY
in January 2012

9 8 7 6 5 4 3 2 1

UNDER the WEATHER

Stories About Climate Change

edited by **Tony Bradman**

F

FRANCES LINCOLN
CHILDREN'S BOOKS

Contents

Introduction

I suppose I first began to think about climate change a few years ago during a particularly warm February. I remember getting in my car to drive to the supermarket at the end of the road, and realizing when I got there that I could have probably done without my thick winter coat. In fact, it was very warm, almost like the kind of day I remembered from the summers of my childhood.

From that moment on, I began to take rather more notice of what was going on around the world. I learned all the terms that we have grown used to – greenhouse gases, carbon footprint, global warming. I watched the news and saw films of freak weather events all round the world, of floods and sea levels rising, of droughts and animals on the brink of extinction because of threats to their habitats. I listened to the debates that raged about what was happening.

But there seemed to be something missing from all this talk – the voices of the people who were being directly affected, particularly children. I wanted to hear how they *felt* about climate change, and I had a feeling that it would all be more complicated than the headlines might lead us to believe. The world is a big place, but everything in it is connected. Small things that happen in one part of the world might have big effects elsewhere – and they are not always bad.

So I decided that the best way to hear those voices was to ask some really good writers to write stories about climate change, focusing on the children of our planet. The result is the book that you're holding, and I think you'll soon see just how complex and difficult an issue climate change is. The stories are set in almost every part of the globe – the UK, Zambia, the USA, Siberia, Canada, the Philippines, Australia, Sri Lanka – and what's interesting is that they're full of surprises – the biggest one for me being that it's not all gloom and doom.

Of course there are problems. In Candy Gourlay's story *How To Build The Perfect Sandcastle* the whole future of an island in the Philippines is threatened by something as seemingly harmless as a one degree rise in sea temperature. In Susan Sandercock's *Sea Canaries* a girl discovers that Beluga whales are also threatened by changes to the sea, and in Karen Ball's haunting *Moonlight* a Sri Lankan family is changed forever because of rising summer temperatures.

But good things emerge despite the changes – perhaps even because of them. Three children round the world make a connection in Francis McCrickard's *As Busy As...* and in Miriam Halahmy's *Tommo and the Bike Train* and George Ivanoff's *Future Dreaming* children realise that they can do something to help save the future, especially if they work together. That might be hard, as the boy in Lily Hyde's story set in Siberia shows us – but it's got to be worth doing if we want to avoid the future that Linda Newbery shows us in *Wasters*.

These stories have certainly set me thinking, anyway. Our world is suffering, so in a sense we're all under the weather. But we don't have to be – the future is ours to change, should we choose to do so.

How to Build the Perfect Sandcastle

by Candy Gourlay

How to Build the Perfect Sandcastle *is loosely based on beautiful Boracay Island in my native Philippines, which has a stunning beach of powder white sand. In 1998, the sea around Boracay became hotter by just one degree. The rise in sea temperature and pollution from uncontrolled development has killed off most of the coral reef that protects its shores. Without the reef, the sand is slowly washing away, into the sea. The islanders have not been quick to seek solutions, and now they are racing against the clock.*

If I told you how to build a perfect sandcastle, I'd have to kill you.

That's a joke. Actually it's easy to build a perfect sandcastle if you live on Sugar Island. Sugar Island has a beach called Sugar Beach. It's called Sugar Beach because the sand really looks like sugar.

Tip: When building a sandcastle bigger than you, start in the middle and work your way outwards.

I don't want to brag but I am amazing at building sandcastles. The tourists hang around watching me, buying me cola and asking stupid questions.

I've been building this really massive castle for just three hours and the tourists have parked themselves all around.

Tip: The half-shell of coconut is perfect
for collecting tips. And the tourists like
it because they think it looks ethnic.

My coconut is already overflowing with coins.

That will show Pa. He doesn't like me building sandcastles for tourists.

"Ben, stay off the beach. Twelve-year-olds belong in school!" he says. "We don't need the money!"

So why does Pa work extra hours at the Green Mango Hotel after spending the whole day taking snorkelling parties out to sea? Why does Ma take in washing as well as making those bead necklaces to sell?

"If you keep bunking school, you'll end up a beach bum like that no-good Peanut!" It's one of Pa's favourite things to yell about. Funny because when I grow up I *want* to be like Peanut.

I don't tell Pa of course. He'd go berserk if he knew.

Peanut's a sculptor. He's got cool dreadlocks and a little beard and makes weird vases and pretty ladies out of clay. He carves driftwood too. Totem poles with monkey-eating eagles and crocodiles and squirrel monkeys.

I figure that when Peanut was ten years old like me, he must have been stupendous at building sandcastles too.

Tip: The best time to build a castle is after a big rain when the sand is moist and sticky.

When it rains on Sugar Island, it rains hard. Last night's rain has totally washed away the path in front of the Sea Coconut Bar. Even the sand around the nearby coconut trees is gone. The trees look naked with their knotty root balls exposed. Oh boy.

The Japanese lady who runs the bar has hired my friend Spit and his pa to pile sand around the coconut trees, rebuild the path and shovel grit all over it. She wants it done pronto.

That's why I am building on Spit's spot. Spit and I have a deal. He does his sandcastles on the stretch between the Sea Coconut Bar and the Banana Boat Station and I do mine between the Banana Boat Station and Life's A Beach ('The One Stop Beach Shop'). But my stretch of beach is a lot grittier. Spit's got sandier sand on his spot.

Spit isn't coming back in a hurry. It should take ages to rebuild that path.

Tip: Use a paintbrush.

The tourists oooh and aaah when I pull out my tools. They think it's so cool that I build castles without a bucket and spade. I use a paintbrush for the design. My favourite is a slice of driftwood I found on the shore, flat and smooth and tapering to a point.

I cut out the words: *Welcome to Sugar Beach!* and they go wild, cheering and clapping, and I turn around and bow like a magician who's just pulled a rabbit out of a hat. They crowd around and snap photos and put more money into my coconut.

Doesn't take long for the tourists to get bored though. Before you know it, they're strolling off to stare at something else on the beach.

"Wheresh Shpit?"

I whirl round to find Peanut swaying behind me, a plank of driftwood under his arm and a bottle of beer in his hand. Oh boy. His voice is slurry and his eyes are red. He sticks an arm around me. His armpit is rank.

"It'sh all going to be gone shoon, you know."

"What's going to be gone?" I push his arm

off my shoulder. I want to be like Peanut when I grow up but not when he is like this.

He laughs, a high pitched huh-huh-huh. "The *shand*! It's washing away! Swoosh, swoosh!"

"The sand?"

Peanut puts his arm around me again. "No more shand! No more Sugar Beach! No more tourishts!"

Whack! Sand sprays the air in a gritty shower.

Whack! Whack! Whack!

Spit's baseball bat hits the castle three more times before I manage to grab his arm. Too late. The castle crumbles like a birthday cake.

"I – told – you – this – part – of – the – beach – is – *mine*!" With every word, Spit jerks his arm, trying to pull free. He's strong, Spit. He's two whole months older than me.

At last, Spit manages to rip his arm from me and the bat swings out uncontrollably.

Whack!

Peanut drops to the sand, unconscious, a trickle of blood on his forehead. Oh boy.

Spit and I stare.

Spit tosses away his bat and shoves me hard on the shoulder. "Look what you've done! He's dead."

Tip: A person who snores is not dead.

Five minutes later and Peanut is still snoring. If I don't go home now, Pa will find out I've bunked school again.

"Do you think he's got brain damage?" I wipe the blood off his forehead with the palm of my hand. There's nothing there but a teeny tiny cut and an impressive blue lump.

"He's already got brain damage." Spit staggers back from the sea with a bucket full of water. "Peanut's already loony."

"What's that for?" I look at the bucket.

"This!" Spit empties the bucket on to Peanut's head.

Peanut sits up, choking and spluttering.

"I've seen it done on TV," Spit says. "Always works!"

"You all right, Peanut?" I peer into Peanut's face. He is blinking like he isn't sure where he is.

"Oh hell. I'm late," he says, his voice no longer slurred. He gets on his feet and, shading his eyes, looks out to sea.

"You better sit down," Spit says loudly, like Peanut is hard of hearing. "You've probably got brain damage."

"I need you fellows to help me lift something," Peanut says.

"We've got to go home," I say. Pa's voice is ringing in my ear. *If I catch you bunking school again...*

"Did I say you had any choice?" Peanut's eyes are sharp. "What's your pa going to say, Spit, when I tell him you hit me with a bat? Huh, I wouldn't want to be there when *your* pa hears what happened, Ben!"

Tip: There's no point protesting
when you want to go anyway.

Peanut's shack is a short way up a sandy trail from the beach. It's just a thing made of planks with a hammock out front. You can barely see it for all the ferns and palms and bushes that Peanut plants around it. His driftwood totems and terracotta urns peek from within the lush greenery like artefacts hidden in the jungle. At night the coconut trees sparkle with all the fairy lights that Peanut winds round the trunks. It's a cool place.

There are several huge terracotta urns on the path, except you couldn't plant a palm in any of them because great big holes are cut into them.

"We need to take these to the boat," says Peanut.

"What for?" Spit and I say at the same time.

"I'm doing some gardening in the sea!" Peanut grins.

Tip: You can make coral grow on stuff you sink into the sea, like old tyres and even shipwrecks. But terracotta urns are a lot better-looking.

It takes us ages because we have to lift the urns on to a sort of sled that Peanut has fashioned out of bamboo and then we have to drag it all the way to Peanut's little outrigger, *The Coral Queen*, which is moored at the bouldery end of the beach.

The urns make the boat sit so low in the water it looks like it would sink if it hadn't been for the long wooden outriggers on either side.

"Well?" Peanut says when we finish loading the boat.

"Well what?" I say.

"Are you kids coming along or going home?"

"I'm coming," says Spit, jumping in. "My pa won't be finished at the Sea Coconut until late."

I close my eyes. I can hear Pa's voice. *You've been bunking school again, haven't you? How many times have I said...*

Peanut is not dawdling. *The Coral Queen* is already out of reach when I make up my mind. I jump into the water and swim for the boat. "Wait for me!"

Tip: No point missing something
if your pa's going to be mad anyway.

"So you're growing a coral garden?" Spit and I crawl out on to the outriggers and make little spurts of sea spray up with our heels as the boat picks up speed.

"I'm growing a coral *reef*," Peanut yells so we can hear him above the motor.

Spit and I look at each other. Spit twirls a finger around his ear. "Loony," he yells.

Sugar Island doesn't need another coral reef. There is a massive reef on the North end of the island where Pa takes his snorkellers. And there is another big one in the South end, where we are headed.

Besides, one man can't build himself a coral reef. Peanut can make the urns, but he'll need thousands. There isn't enough clay on the island to make that many. Oh boy. What a loony.

We stop just within sight of Crocodile Rock which looks more like a dog with a fat tail. Peanut pulls thick ropes out of the boat locker.

"Peanut," I stare at the giant urns. "There can't be any space down there for these. What about the reef that's already there?"

"There isn't anything down there," Peanut says, looping the ropes around the urns. "This reef is dead."

"Dead?" I stare at him.

"You're kidding, right, Peanut? The reef isn't dead," Spit says.

Peanut looks annoyed. "What, you think I'm loony or something?"

Both of us look away.

Peanut throws us a couple of snorkels and masks from the boat locker. "Dive in. Go on. Take a look. The reef is dead."

We dive.

I've gone with Pa on his trips to the North reef many times. The tourists don't mind me snorkelling with them, swimming right down to see the underwater blooms, the clouds of rainbow-coloured fish flitting in and out of the coral branching out from the ocean floor like a flower garden.

That's not what it's like here. No way is this a flower garden. It's more like a disaster zone, like someone dropped a bomb into the sea and blasted away all the coral. It lies broken on the ocean floor, like a million shards of china. The water is still and blue and silent. There are no fish. It is a graveyard. Oh boy.

When Spit and I surface, Peanut has finished getting the urns ready. We help him drop them into the deep, each sinking swiftly to the bottom. When all the urns are gone, we are silent.

I am the first one to speak. "What happened, Peanut? When did the reef die?"

Peanut squints at me. "Remember two years ago?"

I shake my head.

"Two years ago, the whole world experienced some really high temperatures. Underwater, it was hot too. The sea temperature rose by one degree. It killed the reef."

Spit leans forward. "But the North reef's OK, right? The snorkel people go there every day."

Peanut stubs his cigarette out in the sardine can he uses as an ashtray. "Not for long. It's still hot in there. The coral is bleaching. Not long before the North reef is dead too."

Tip: Without reefs, there is nothing to protect Sugar Beach from the weather. So sand gets washed away. Soon there will be no more Sugar Beach. No Sugar Beach means no tourists. No tourists mean no work. No work means no Sugar Island.

Spit and I are silent on the way back. We are trying to imagine what a beach would look like without any sand.

There are two small figures on the boulders when we near Sugar Island. As we get closer, I recognise my pa and Spit's pa and my heart sinks. Pa must be really cross if he's come here instead of reporting for work at the Green Mango.

They start yelling before we're even close enough to tie up the boat. But they're not yelling at us. They're yelling at Peanut.

"What were you thinking taking two boys

out with you to sea?"...

..."What if something happened?"...

..."It's kidnapping! We could have called the police!"...

Peanut is yelling too.

"They helped me drop some coral domes for the reef. That's more than any islander's ever done!"

Pa grabs my arm and begins to lead me away. "Don't you dare talk to me like that, Peanut. You're nothing but a drunk!"

"And you're an ostrich with your head in the sand – except at this rate there won't be any sand left to hide in!"

Spit is scrambling after his pa up the rocks to his house on the other side of the island. "Pa! Pa! We were just helping Peanut rebuild the reef."

But Spit's pa just marches on without saying anything.

"Pa," I say. "Did you know the South reef is dead?"

Pa doesn't answer.

"You knew, didn't you?" I whisper but I am sure he can hear me. The evening is quiet save for the low swish of the coconut trees in the breeze.

"Everybody knows!" Peanut yells and Pa stops walking. "But it's a secret, isn't it?"

"A secret?" I look from one man to the other. "How can it be a secret if everybody knows?"

Pa bows his head.

Peanut grabs Pa's shoulder and turns him so that they are looking each other in the eye.

"It's Everybody's secret because Everybody doesn't want the world to know. Everybody thinks the *tourists* will stop coming if they knew."

Pa opens his mouth to say something but doesn't. He turns and walks up the trail without looking back and I have no choice but to follow him. We walk home in total silence.

That night there is a storm. The windows shudder like they're freezing cold and I can hear the sea groaning and raging under the howling of the wind. There are crashing sounds outside.

As I lie in my bed I imagine giant waves chewing at the shore, eating up all that sugar-white sand an entire dune at a time. I creep into Ma and Pa's room. Pa's eyes are open. I climb under their sheet and into Pa's arms and he holds me tight as we listen until the banging and screaming of the storm calms to a murmur.

It is early in the morning but everyone is out on the beach when Pa and I go out to see what damage the storm has done.

Everywhere there are coconut shells and palm fronds that have been ripped out of the trees. A tree blew on to the roof of the Green Mango Hotel. The Banana Boat Station has lost its thatch and the Sea Coconut Bar has lost its path again. The coconut trees look silly with their roots exposed, like they've lost their skirts.

Everywhere I hear voices reporting what has been lost, blown away or crushed by the storm.

The beach looks smaller.

There is a terrible moaning sound from the

far end of the beach. It rises louder and louder. Someone is crying.

Pa and I run across the sand. Is there someone in need of help?

It is Peanut, his dreadlocks a wild tangle over his eyes. He is on his knees, weeping in the sand with his arms around something.

It's a broken piece of his coral garden. All along the beach, bobbing slightly in the shallows, orange fragments of his urns lie scattered. The storm has broken them up. There is going to be no coral reef.

Pa gently takes the fragment from Peanut and puts his arms around him.

"It's all gone!" Peanut weeps on to Pa's shoulder. "It took me months to make them."

"There, there," Pa whispers.

"It's over," Peanut sobs. "I can't do it any more. I can't do it. I'm nothing. I'm just one man."

A tear trickles down my cheek. I can still see the devastation on the ocean floor. The coral broken and lifeless in that blue, dead place.

"Peanut, you're not alone," Pa says. "You're right. We can't keep it a secret any longer."

Tip: In the end, you've got to do what's right for the future, even if it's a long, long time away. Like going to school instead of bunking off to earn pennies on the beach. Like doing something about the reef instead pretending it isn't happening.

At first it is only Pa. He helps Peanut put more coral urns on the seabed. But the sea keeps spitting them out.

So Spit's pa joins them, trying to figure something out.

And then the Japanese lady from the Sea Coconut Bar comes along. And then the folks at the Banana Boat Station. And the Green Mango Hotel. And pretty soon all the islanders are talking and thinking and trying to figure something out. Oh boy.

Tip: Stuff is less scary when there is more than one of you.

And of course the answer is out there.

But the answer doesn't come cheaply. You need scientists and experts and equipment.

And even all the islanders together don't have that kind of money.

Tip: Sometimes you just have to ask.

It's me who thinks of something in the end.

I don't want to brag but I am amazing at building sandcastles.

So I say, I'm going to build a sandcastle.

I start in the middle and work my way outward.

Spit joins in.

And Pa helps too.

And so does Spit's pa. And Peanut. And the Japanese lady from the Sea Coconut Bar. And . . . well, everybody helps.

Next thing we know, we've built the most enormous, massive, GIGANTIC, humongous sandcastle. The tourists are so excited they can barely applaud.

"Coconuts!" I yell. And everybody runs around grabbing coconuts. We put a hundred coconuts out for the tourists to fill. And guess what, the tourists fill them up and more.

Then helicopters arrive with newspaper and TV people to see the biggest sandcastle ever built. And they learn about how the hot sea has killed the reef. So they go back to their newspapers and TV stations and tell the world about it.

Next thing we know the world is sending us some money to help. And scientists. And experts.

And equipment.

Next thing we know the coral reefs around the island are slowly but surely growing back.

So Sugar Beach is safe. Which means Sugar Island's safe. Which means we are, all of us, safe.

Oh boy.

Sea Canaries

by Susan Sandercock

Jess is an ordinary girl on an extraordinary whale-watching trip in Manitoba, Canada, when she becomes enchanted by wild belugas and it changes her life.

I wrote this story after seeing beluga whales in Vancouver Aquarium whilst on holiday in Canada. After researching them on the internet, I was shocked to discover the heart-breaking plight of these animals due to climate change.

I've tried to give a real sense of the whales, and how awesomely beautiful they are. Their underwater songs are a feast for the senses, and I hope the belugas in my story inspire you as much as they have inspired me.

Jess's hair flapped in the sharp sub-arctic wind as she rubbed her hands together. *It's never as cold as this back home in Kent,* she thought, as her group's whale-watching jet-boat tore through the murky waters of the Churchill River.

Pods of gleaming white beluga whales broke the skin of the water. "Wow!" she said, for the zillionth time that day. She'd thought their first week in Canada, in Vancouver and the Rockies, had been great but Manitoba was excellent. She'd never been so excited in her life; it was as if a huge wave was swelling inside her chest. The large beluga pod followed them, diving and splashing through the water, their black eyes fixed on the boat, chirping like they were trying to speak. She laughed as they sprayed water from their blowholes – splashing her elbow – as their plump dolphin-like bodies arched through the jade-green water.

"Dad, can we come here every year?" Jess asked.

"No, we can't, cheeky," Mum cut in before

Dad had a chance to reply. "This Canadian tour is to celebrate your first year at grammar school. We can't afford to make a habit of it." Jess could tell she was in one of her serious moods, because a vein that lay flat most of the time in the side of her forehead was twitching. "You'll have to keep up those high grades next year, too."

Jess nodded, although she could already feel the wave inside her crashing, the water fizzling away. Anyway, she knew the truth; the belugas' lives, like hers, weren't easy. She'd read all about it on the Internet. The sub-arctic ice was melting and making the sea less salty, which was causing the fish on which belugas feed to die.

"You'll have to improve on English for next year, though," Mum said. "I had a chat with Miss Miller, she told me the reason you only got a B in your report is because your punctuation isn't spot on. As soon as we get home, you'll have to practise, little and often, every night; no more going round to Rosie's for your dinner on Thursdays."

"Mum!" Jess squealed.

"Your mother's right," Dad said, although he looked a bit uncomfortable; he always backed Mum up when she got like this.

Mum slapped the side of the boat. "Come ten years' time, you'll be at the front of a courtroom!"

Jess sighed. She was sick of hearing the story of how Mum and Dad met at uni when they were both studying law, but failed to make it as practising lawyers. When Jess was younger, they'd been watching one of the soaps on TV and a courtroom scene had come up. She'd made the mistake of saying it would be cool to work with criminals. Mum had exclaimed she was delighted her daughter wanted to follow her shattered dream, and had never let it drop. It didn't help that Jess excelled at all the practical subjects at school, and liked facts and figures. Mum was convinced it was 'meant to be' and Dad cautiously agreed with her.

The belugas lolled in the water, some stuck

up their heads. Dad and the other three tourists in their party pulled out their cameras. One beluga made chattering bird-like noises. "That's why they're nicknamed sea canaries," she heard Hank, their driver and onboard marine biologist, say to someone.

Jess dangled her hands over the edge of the boat, although the whales weren't quite close enough to touch. Jess loved her parents and didn't want to disappoint them, and of course she was grateful they'd brought her on this trip – even though it heaped up the pressure to continue getting good grades. She loved nature. When she was little, and Mum and Dad used to take her into the woods, she'd enjoyed identifying wildflowers. Last week in Vancouver, she'd borrowed a passer-by's binoculars so she could admire the bald eagles perching high in the treetops. In the Rockies, she'd hidden in the forest for hours with Dad to photograph some elk, and had been the only one to spot a grizzly bear from the tour bus window.

Before this trip, she'd read up about belugas on the Internet. The ocean had never been a specific interest of hers, but the research had fascinated her – and upset her.

"I told you they were curious, didn't I?" Hank wound an underwater microphone called a hydrophone into the sea. Jess heard the crackle of the river and the belugas singing underwater.

A huge adult beluga bobbed out of the water and stared at the red-brown rocks of the shoreline. All the other members of her group were smiling broadly, their faces pink and shiny. Dad was getting snappy with the camera. Even Mum was more relaxed; the vein in her forehead had stopped quivering.

Everyone was "ooh-ing" and "ah-ing", enjoying the day one hundred percent. Nobody realised what life was really like for the belugas. Until Jess had done her research, she just hadn't realised whales were so affected by climate change. Polar bears and penguins, yes, they lived on the ice. But how many people really knew of the whales' plight? They looked happy. Jess couldn't imagine them struggling to search out depleted supplies of krill.

An adult beluga turned its head around like it could tell she was thinking about them. Another thing she'd discovered was belugas are the only whales that have moveable neck vertebrae.

Hank sidled up to her. "Cute, isn't it? Although he looks a bit silly. You like him?"

Jess nodded.

"He's the grandfather of the pod."

"How do you know that?"

"I keep a close eye on these guys," Hank scanned the estuary with his binoculars. "They come back every year and I get to know them pretty well."

Through the hydrophone speakers, many belugas were singing in a complex concerto. It sounded ghostlike. "I like how they sing," Jess said. "It's a shame their lives aren't easy."

Hank turned to her. "These guys are pretty happy here. They come every year for the capelin fish, there's always plenty for them to eat."

"That's good," Jess was relieved. "But other belugas aren't so lucky, are they? They can't all swim here."

"I guess not, no."

"Climate change is ruining their lives."

Hank sucked air through his teeth. "Ooh, the biggie. Like I said, they're OK in the estuary over the summer, it's when they head into the open sea they're at risk. Less food, and less ice for foraging."

Jess had heard of the problems of less foraging space. It meant the belugas could be snatched more easily from the sea by predators – perhaps by an opportune polar bear.

An inquisitive beluga nudged the raft and everyone laughed. Hank turned to her when the wobbling stopped. "And then there's ocean acidification."

Jess frowned. "What's that?"

"The one with the potential to do the most damage. Fighter plankton live in the ocean and absorb carbon dioxide in the same way trees do on land. In fact, they absorb more than trees do. But we're throwing more at the ocean than it can handle, which eventually means no oxygen for coral and fish, and therefore no food for whales."

Jess stared at a pair of belugas playfully nudging heads whilst Hank paused for breath.

"Yes, the belugas are better off here than anywhere else, but in other parts of Canada beluga numbers are dropping. If the ocean fails to absorb all our carbon dioxide, fifty percent of our oxygen supply will go, and then it won't just be entire whale species becoming extinct – it will be us." Another person from their party asked Hank a question and he edged away from her. "Nice talking to you."

Jess stared at the frolicking, chattering belugas. The knowledge that one day they wouldn't be playing here at all terrified her.

To make matters worse, it wasn't just the belugas that were dying; the ocean itself was under threat.

Hank zoomed them back to shore and she watched the flat, dry sub-arctic tundra appear. *If the ocean stops working, whales will die.*

She couldn't let Mum and Dad pressure her into becoming a lawyer. To save whales – and humans – the ocean needed her help.

✿   ✿   ✿

In the evening, over dinner in the restaurant at their motel, Jess broke the news to her stunned parents. "I don't want to become a lawyer. I never have. I want to be a marine biologist when I'm older."

The vein on Mum's forehead throbbed so hard that Jess wondered if she'd explode. "For goodness sake, what's got into you?

A *marine biologist*? Let me get this straight; you want to spend hours on end working for a pittance in a dingy research lab, living on tiny grants compiling heaps of paperwork, travelling to the ends of the earth in horrible conditions. And it isn't even as though fish can *thank* you. It's ridiculous. What's brought this on?"

"Well, Hank told me –"

"What did he say to scare you like this?" Dad cut in, struggling to put on his calming voice. Jess knew he agreed with Mum really.

"He didn't scare me, just made me face facts." She had to make them see. "Anyway, it wasn't just what he told me. This is my decision. I knew before we came here that climate change is a big problem, but until I spoke to Hank I didn't realise how bad it is. I have to do something."

"What do you mean?" Mum snapped.

"I mean…" It was hard to explain, she was only just understanding herself. "I've always liked flowers, and birds, haven't I? And last week in the Rockies, it was great to see that grizzly bear and all those elk. I really love the ocean. I want to work with marine animals – they're at risk, and so is the ocean itself."

"You sound like you've swallowed a textbook," Mum said. "Except you don't know what you're talking about. I watched a documentary a few weeks ago about this climate change business. It's a load of rubbish. Apparently the earth is warming up naturally. It goes through these phases. Remember, we've already had the dinosaurs and the ice age."

"How can you be so *stupid*?" Jess didn't care that other people were beginning to notice the argument. "Even if it is a natural process, we're speeding it up. We're forcing more carbon dioxide at the ocean than it can handle!"

"Keep your voice down, Jessica!" Dad snapped. Even he looked angry now.

Mum regarded her steadily. "I wish we'd never brought you here," she said in a sad whisper. "I give up with you, I really do."

Jess felt cold all the way through. Her biggest

fear had been that one day she'd disappoint her parents. Now it had happened.

"Fine!" she bellowed, as she stood up. "Be like that! Believe there's nothing we can do. Carry on spending ages in the shower every day, driving the car into town. Murder some more whales. Murder yourself – because that's what will happen!"

She was too angry to care that the restaurant had fallen silent. She ran to their room and threw herself on to the bed. She pulled the pillow tightly over her face until all she saw were icy white stars. A knock on the door, muffled by feathers. "Go away!"

"Jess, it's Dad."

The door squeaked open.

"Jess, please listen to me."

She stared into the white blurry pillowcase, imagining white-blue ice floes, the milky bodies of the belugas.

Dad pulled the pillow away.

"Your mother and I thought you'd like it

here," he said.

"I do," Jess noticed how tight his brow was. "It's great."

"I know you think your mother goes on at you, and maybe she does a bit – sometimes. But we both want what's best for you. Everything is so expensive nowadays. A steady, well-paid career is more important than ever."

"So it's got nothing to do with you both wanting to live through me?"

Dad sighed. "Your mum believes becoming a marine biologist isn't the safest bet, and I happen to agree. But all we really want is for you to be happy."

"Well, I'm not happy." As soon as Jess said it, she knew it was true. *But I would be if I could make you see how important this is to me.* Now she'd seen the whales and learned about them, something had filled a gap in her life that she hadn't even realised had been there. If only she could help the whales *and* please her parents.

"Oh, Jess." Dad took a deep breath. "I believe

mankind will find an answer to this climate change business. That the damage we've done can be sorted. I have great faith in that."

"You really believe if you sit back and do nothing, then it will be OK?"

"There's nothing one person can do." He rose from the bed, indicating the conversation was over. Soon enough, she heard him leave.

Jess burrowed back underneath her pillow. When they came up, much later, she pretended to be asleep. She stared into the darkness under the covers, felt the cold patches with her feet like the belugas must in the ocean with their fins, and whilst the doomed animals uttered music she uttered the muffled human noise of tears.

✿   ✿   ✿

Hank soared their tiny raft out of the river and into the open waters of Hudson Bay. Jess shifted a little and accidentally elbowed Mum.

"Watch it, Jess." Mum was as pale as the belugas; she had never liked swimming in open water and was nervous about the snorkelling. It was making her foul mood worse.

"Liz, please," Dad said. "Not in public."

Jess's anger faded to irritation. If she wanted them both to see how important climate change was, she had to show them on this holiday. If she waited until they caught the train to Toronto later in the week, they'd have forgotten all about this.

"OK, we're here," Hank anchored the raft in place. "Listen carefully to the boring safety talk, please."

Hank explained the final part of their whale-watching experience – entering the water one-by-one to experience a close encounter with the belugas. He held up the long rope that trailed from their raft and explained that the currents were strong and they *must* hold on to it the whole time they were underwater.

The belugas were inquisitive, like cats, and would come very close to them but would not attack. Yes, they *could* touch them.

When he asked who would like to go first, Jess jumped at the chance. She slid on her snorkel, gripped the rope tightly and dropped into the water.

Submerged, she opened her eyes and through the greenish glow she heard the sea canaries singing. Their lilting sounds filled the ocean in a complex orchestra. As her eyes grew accustomed to the murky water, she saw them – four white cylindrical shapes that glowed eerily in the dim light.

She pulled out her snorkel and whispered her own cooing noises to them. Soon, a beluga swam closer, until it was staring into her goggles with its black eyes. She reached out to touch it, but it was gone. She blinked and stared into the suddenly empty space in front of her, and pushed to the surface of the water.

"You were down there for over two minutes!"

Hank said.

"She was born with gills," Dad joked. "How was it, Jess?"

"Amazing," Jess breathed, as they helped her back into the raft.

"OK," Hank said. "Who's next?"

"My wife," Dad said, with a wicked grin.

"No!" Mum waved her hands. "I'll go last. I'm not really sure it's such a good idea, after all. I might pass altogether."

"You'll be fine." Jess patted Mum's shoulder. Maybe if she could make her see how beautiful the whales are, she might be more sympathetic to their predicament. "Go on, you'll enjoy it."

Mum slid towards the edge of the raft, hesitantly. "Not if I've got to put my head under the water."

"That's the whole idea. Don't be such a wimp!" Jess said.

"Fine, I'll do it," Mum gripped the rope tightly and pushed herself over the edge and into the sea. She bobbed there for what seemed like ages.

"Go on, Mum! Other people want their turn, too."

Mum ducked her head under and, to Jess's surprise, stayed there for a good few seconds. She briefly emerged, smiling, before ducking down again. Jess watched the white shapes of the belugas under the surface of the water, her mum's snorkel at the top of the ocean all the time. She watched as Mum reached out and touched the smooth face of a whale. Everyone gasped. Mum's head sprung out of the water. She was grinning widely.

"I actually touched one!" she cried. "It was amazing. It felt so smooth. It was brilliant! Absolutely amazing! Did you get a photo?"

"Yes," Dad said, patting his camera.

Dad and Hank helped her back into the boat.

Mum turned to Jess slowly. "The belugas here, they will be OK, won't they?"

"If they stick close to the estuary they will.

If they wander further out into Hudson Bay, they might not be, because there's less food and less foraging space. In other parts of Canada, and the world, belugas are in serious trouble."

"That's really awful, the poor things." Mum squeezed water from her hair and glanced at Jess. "Sorry I've been a bit off with you. I didn't mean to be."

"It's OK."

"No, it was wrong."

"We're both sorry." Dad glanced away and watched another member of their group descend the rope into the ocean.

There was never going to be a better time to push her point forward. "Swimming with the whales has been the best part of our holiday so far. It wouldn't have been the same without them."

"You can say that again. It was just the most incredible experience." Mum regarded Jess steadily. "OK, sweetie, you win. You taught your father and me something. We'll switch off the heating in the evenings. We'll try to cut down on how often we use the car. Satisfied?"

Jess couldn't help it. "Not quite."

"We'll make a donation to a marine charity of your choice," Dad said in the joking and relaxed tone he always used when they were coming to the end of an argument.

"Giving money to a charity only helps for a little while." Jess refused to be swayed away from the seriousness of it all yet. "It doesn't help in the long term. That's why I want to become a marine biologist when I'm older – so I can really make a difference to the future of all marine animals. You won't change my mind."

Mum took a deep breath and Jess hugged herself, anticipating a new row. She was relieved when Mum shrugged. "OK, if that's what you want. I suppose it's not a bad life being a scientist nowadays. You can even get on the TV; there's always an environment programme on. And you'll become the first person ever in our family to get a PhD. Imagine that! Dr Jessica

Emily Watson!"

Jess rolled her eyes. Mum was off again. But at least this time, she wasn't going all dreamy about her being stuffed inside a boring courtroom all day long. At least this time, she was right behind the cause, and what Jess wanted.

Jess closed her eyes against the sharp wind and let her mind wander back to her time in the water with the sea canaries, until all she heard was the complex music of their chatter under the heavy sheets of water.

As Busy As...

by Francis McCrickard

Britain; Zambia; the USA: the story takes place in all three. The effects of climate change are not confined to one country. It affects us all. Perhaps the three children in this story will grow to understand that we need to take more care of our world including its bees.

When I was a child, there were meadows close to my home. We spent all the long summer days in them. There was loud music played by thousands of bees. Flowers of many colours danced to this music. Recently, I stood in a wildflower meadow and listened and heard only faint music.

Flat on his stomach in the long grass, Joseph pulled himself forward using his elbows. He was a special agent on a secret mission deep in enemy territory. Many people's lives depended on him. Failure was not an option.

"That's far enough, class. Now stay as still as you can and watch closely."

They were sending in Apache Attack helicopters. The aircraft flew fast and low, then hovered, seeking Joseph out. One of them was landing.

"It's collecting nectar from the flower. That's a harebell."

Joseph watched the Apache Attack helicopter almost disappear into the harebell.

The whole of Year Six and Miss Sanderson were lying on their stomachs at the edge of the school wildflower garden they had sown the autumn before.

"What's nectar, Miss?"

"A sugary liquid that the bee makes honey from. Look, can you see that little stick-thing on its head?"

Joseph loved honey. He watched the long-barrelled gun of the Apache Attack helicopter going into another flower.

"That's its *proboscis*; its tongue. It's a thin tube that the bee uses to collect the nectar. Then it carries the nectar back to the hive in its stomach and puts it in the honeycomb. It's food for the bee and its young and it's food for us."

"What are the little yellow sacks I can see on its legs?"

"Ah, well spotted. On its back legs. The bee collects *pollen* in those sacks."

Miss Sanderson bent the stem of one of the flowers that hadn't got a bee on it and pointed inside its petals.

"See these bits?"

She touched the anthers with her little finger and showed them the fine yellow dust.

"That's pollen. The *anthers* are the male bit of the flower and when the bee goes to other harebells, some of the pollen is wiped off its legs and on to this bit of the flower." She pointed inside the flower again. "That's the female bit, the *stigma*. And that's how seeds and fruits and vegetables are made. It's called *pollination* and it's very important. A lot of our food comes from pollination. If the bees and other insects and birds and the wind didn't spread the pollen, we wouldn't have much to eat."

Joseph aimed his high velocity finger at one of the bees that had settled on a tall ox-eye daisy. He squeezed the trigger. The bee flew off and the flower shuddered. Joseph edged backwards slowly through the grass – mission accomplished.

All the class enjoyed watching the DVD again. Miss Sanderson had said they could because it was such a cold and dull February day and everyone needed to be reminded that soon the weather would change, the wildflower garden would start to show its beautiful colours once more and the bees would be busy again.

The following morning at breakfast, Joseph

held the spoon high above the plate and tried to draw patterns with the dripping honey on his toast. He wanted to make a capital J but the honey was so runny that it trickled everywhere and the J was more like an A when he finished. With the back of the spoon, Joseph spread the honey to all the four edges of the bread. He always did this before taking his first bite.

Joseph loved honey and loved the fact that Apache Attack helicopters make it. He had eaten lavender honey from Yorkshire; orchard honey from Herefordshire; clover honey from West Wales; heather honey from Scotland; orange blossom honey from Mexico and eucalyptus honey from Argentina. The honey was still dripping from his spoon but missed his toast and his plate and the table and dribbled down the front of his school shirt. It was almond blossom honey that his Auntie Helen brought him from California.

✿　✿　✿

Daisy Brenkle climbed out of the pick-up and scanned the orchard that covered one side of the gently sloping Californian valley. She followed her father, running to keep up with his long, confident stride, as he zigzagged among the almond trees. Daisy wanted him to stop. She had something important to tell him. This was one of the best days in the year, the day the first almond flowers opened on the thousands of trees on their California farm. She loved this day, especially the beauty of the blossom, but this year it was different. The blossom was early and something was missing.

"Pop, please ... slow down!" She gripped his belt with both hands and dug her heels into the dirt, "Whoah!"

Frank Brenkle pulled his daughter for a few more steps and then stopped and turned. "Daisy, I have work to do. What is it?"

"Listen, Pop. Listen."

Frank stood still for a moment. They looked down the rows of trees. The branches were the usual blizzard of white, but it was quiet, too quiet.

"Where are the bees, Pop?"

It was as if she had hit her father with a hammer. Now he listened, listened hard. There should be wild bees around; there always were before they brought in the hives. Frank had heard of this problem but had ignored it. That was his nature. Everything would turn out OK in the end. His stride was different now. He walked on quickly, but with short, stuttering steps, almost stumbling at times. Daisy sat against the trunk of one of the trees. She heard her father talking to himself at the top of his voice.

"Can't hear a thing! Not one of them! Never thought to listen before! Stupid! Not a buzz ... can't be ... not one."

Fifteen minutes later, he returned to where Daisy was. She stood up and shielded her eyes from the sun.

"When are the hives coming, Pop?"

"Bill Campbell's on his way, Daisy, but *he's*

got problems too." Frank Brenkle sat down beside his daughter. "I've been burying my head in the sand, Daisy. Something's happening. Something's changing."

✧   ✧   ✧

Emmanuel Chinunda walked slowly to school in the middle of the riverbed. There was only a trickle of water. At the start of the rainy season, things had looked good with regular, steady rain each day. Then, the drought had come and it had been a terrible growing season. If rain didn't fall soon, there would be very little to harvest. The crops, especially maize, were already wasting. Emmanuel's family still had food but supplies were getting low. There had been bad years before in their village in Zambia, years when the family went hungry for weeks, but his father said that this year was the worst.

"I can't read the sky any more."

Emmanuel's mother had given him a nickname: *nkulumushi*, the blue lizard. She called him this because the lizard runs in straight lines quickly and so it was with her son. He made up his mind quickly and did things without too much thought. After school, Emmanuel ran home. Something sweet would cheer everyone up. An uncle had told him stories of bee-hunters who went deep into the forest to find hives and came back with buckets full of honey. He knew it was no good to simply search. You could hunt all day and lose your way without finding the precious treasure. Some people followed a bird, the honey-guide, but Emmanuel didn't know that bird. There was another way.

Emmanuel took the small, wooden box with the hinged door that he and his sisters used to keep mice in. Then, he found a large, empty milk powder tin, punched two holes just below the rim and fastened a string handle through the holes. There was one more thing to do and then he was ready to hunt.

Emmanuel put sugar on the tin lid and added a little hot water. He put the box on its side so that the door was on top, placed the lid inside and carried them to his parents' garden. The bees were busiest among the squashes and pumpkins and that's where he placed the box. Very quickly they swarmed over the sugar syrup on the lid. When Emmanuel saw that plenty of them were inside, he closed the lid and trapped the bees.

He took a deep breath and, carefully, opened the lid a fraction and allowed one bee to get out. He watched closely as it rose, made a circle and then flew east along the river towards Emmanuel's school. Emmanuel ran after it carrying the box of angry, buzzing bees. He quickly lost sight of that first bee but he knew it had gone just beyond the school at the back of Mr. Pikiti's store. Emmanuel released another bee and did the same, running and watching until it was out of sight and then walking to the last point he had seen it. He was so excited and so keen to find honey, that he didn't realise how long the hunt was taking and how low the sun was getting. He followed the bees past St Charles Lwanga church, two miles along the bank of the river and then away from the river, past Masongola village. Emmanuel was off the forest paths now. Thorn bushes pulled at his clothes and scratched his skin. The bees led him up Isubilo Hill where long ago a battle had been fought between his tribe and people from the south. He released another bee at the top and it led him down the slope to meet the river again after it wound slowly around the foot of the hill.

When Emmanuel had released seventeen bees, he found the hive. He was in a part of the forest that he had never seen before, and he felt a little anxious. His parents might be looking for him. His father would be angry. He should have helped them in the garden that afternoon. He looked at the sun; there was perhaps an hour and a half before the dark drew its curtain quickly over the land.

Emmanuel released the rest of the bees and

they disappeared inside a hole high in a baobab, the tree that God had thrown out of his garden. It had landed upside down, its roots in the air, but still grew. There were no branches close to the ground that Emmanuel could pull himself up by. He sharpened short sticks with his knife and pushed them into the soft bark making footholds to get him up into the branches. When he had enough footholds, he climbed back down, picked clumps of dry grass, twisted them into several tight bundles along with some green vegetation, pushed them inside the belt that held up his shorts and climbed back up with his milk powder tin.

The bees raged as if they knew someone was about to disturb their home. Emmanuel lit one of the twists of grass and held it over the hole. The green leaves made a lot of smoke which Emmanuel blew into the hive. At first he didn't think it was going to work and the smoke made him cough. After he had used four of the twists of grass, he saw that the smoke had calmed the bees and he reached in carefully for the honey. He should have used another twist. A bee stung his hand and he pulled it back quickly but he was so excited to have found the hive and to be so close to harvesting honey for his family that he didn't care. He thrust his hand back again; another bee stung his arm as he tore the honeycomb apart and crammed it into the tin.

✿   ✿   ✿

Three huge trucks bumped along the track at the side of the orchard to the picnic area where the hives were brought every year. Bill Campbell climbed down from the first of them.

Daisy liked Bill. He was a very large but gentle man who did everything slowly and steadily. He never rushed like her father. Bill brought his hives each year and he always called Daisy his California Flower. After Bill had lifted, twirled and put Daisy back on the ground again, he shook Frank's hand.

"I've brought you all I have, but it's just over half the hives I had last year. Don't understand it. The bees have vanished, except for a few that are dead."

"Disease?"

"Could be or it could be pollution and the weather swings we're having. It's getting harder to say just when the blossom's coming. The bees get confused, don't know when winter's finishing and spring's starting. They've got to get their timing right and if they don't, they've no food and no strength to fight diseases any more."

Bill pushed his hat back and scratched his head. Daisy noticed beads of sweat and a red line across his forehead. "And I'll be honest with you, Frank. I don't even know if there's still bees in all these hives I've brought. Wouldn't surprise me if we found more of them empty when we lift them down."

Bill's crew started rapidly unloading the hundreds of hives. When they had finished and Bill and his trucks had left, Frank Brenkle walked to the nearest tree and looked up into the web of branches. Daisy was sitting on the lowest bough. She had placed a sprig of blossom in her long, brown hair. Usually, this would have made her father smile, but it didn't and Daisy saw that he was worried.

"I don't think there's enough," he said. "Those bees won't pollinate all our trees."

Daisy lay awake that night. The door to her room was open and her parents' voices drifted upstairs to her. That noise had always comforted her through her childhood. It was a settling end to *her* day; her mother and father talking quietly about *their* day. That evening the voices didn't help her settle. They were arguing, her father telling her mother that she was exaggerating and her mother telling her father that he wasn't facing up to facts.

"We could be ruined," she said, "not this

year, but next maybe."

"We'll see," said her father.

✧　✧　✧

The day following his honey-hunt was a very special one at Emmanuel's school. It was the day the laptop computer arrived. Six months earlier, a teacher, Mrs Sanderson of Water Street School in England, had visited Chilabula School in order to establish links with her primary school in Britain. She had stayed for three weeks and had brought a lot of gifts from the children she taught. The laptop was another gift.

Mr Mulenga, the head teacher, told the class at assembly that the laptop would be used to help them learn and also to communicate with the children of Water Street Primary in Britain. Emmanuel's class was the top class in the school and it would have use of the laptop.

Their assignment for that day was to write to Water Street School thanking everyone for this wonderful gift. Each child would be given the name of an English child in the top class in Water Street and they would e-mail that child. Emmanuel was given the name, *Joseph Watson.* When it was his turn, Emmanuel wrote to Joseph telling him about his family and about how, the day before, he had followed the bees and found the honey and, even though his parents had been angry because it was almost dark when he returned home, he was going to go back for more. Emmanuel liked writing English and wrote more than the other children in his class. He wondered if Joseph liked honey. Was there honey in England? Had Joseph ever hunted for honey? Were there birds in England that would show Joseph where the hives were? He, Emmanuel was going to find out about those birds because following them must be easier than releasing and following bees.

"There is rain to the north, heavy rain,

and it should come our way," said Emmanuel's father with a smile like a… What was the saying the class had learned in English today? *Like a Cheshire cat*! His father had a smile like a Cheshire cat.

Emmanuel had a strange dream that night. He dreamt the rains had come but the forest was on fire. When he spoke of the dream, his father frowned.

"That is not a good dream," he said, and left home to work in the garden, shouting, "Next, I'll be dreaming that a rat crosses my path! Now, that would bring bad luck!"

Three days later, Chilabula village did not exist. The rains came suddenly in the hills to the west of the village and spread over the whole region, rains like people had never seen before, heavy, hard drops that hurt you. Everyone scurried for home but no one's thatched roof kept out this rain totally. It penetrated, dampening everything and snuffing out fires. At first the people were happy. They laughed and joked with each other, shouting to make themselves heard over the din of the rain: "This will make the crops grow!"

A sound, like a growl from a creature bigger than any that roamed the African forests, was the only warning the people were given before the deluge hit the village. Like a great brush, the river water swept everything in front of it, trees, houses, furniture, animals, people...

The river had risen so high that it spilled well over its banks, and flooded the road into the village. The first police Land Rover coming to the disaster got stuck in mud. It wasn't until the following morning that the police and army units that had rushed from the capital to Chilabula were able to see the extent of the destruction and estimate how many villagers had been killed or were missing. Emmanuel Chinunda was among those missing.

✿　✿　✿

"I know where Emmanuel is," Joseph said after Miss Sanderson had told the children in her class what had happened.

Miss Sanderson smiled. Joseph had a great imagination. He probably thought that one of those helicopters he's always talking about had picked Emmanuel out of the flood.

"He could be in the upside-down tree," he said.

"Joseph, this is very serious. You mustn't joke about it."

✿ ✿ ✿

One minute, the riverbed was quiet and almost empty of water; the next, a huge wave of water bullied its way along the channel, spilling over the great flat rocks at the edges and charging in all directions into the forest like a schoolyard emptying of children. It blundered among the trees, pushing, hitting, and quickly knocking over the smaller, younger ones, and trying to climb Isubilo Hill. The roots of the mature trees, like huge arms, flexed their muscles to halt the flow but it was in vain. Some trees stood firm but others were torn from the ground like flowers and carried swiftly in the flow.

The flood reached the baobab and swirled about the base of the broad trunk. Emmanuel clung to a bough with arms and legs. The tree did not move. It had seen off bullies many times before in the thousand years of its existence and it wasn't going to let this one get the better of it. Emmanuel sensed the tree's confidence and knew he would survive. From his perch, he watched the swollen river, murky with soil and choked with debris, surging past him. He recognised parts of houses drifting by. He saw desks from his school; he saw plants that had been uprooted from gardens; he saw dead cattle and chickens; dead wild animals; he saw dead people.

✿   ✿   ✿

"They could try looking there, Miss."

Mr Mulenga, the head teacher of Chilabula School had sent an e-mail to say that all of the pupils were safe except for Emmanuel Chinunda who was still missing. Miss Sanderson gave in and wrote back.

"Can you give them directions, Joseph, on how to get to the tree?"

Joseph could. Emmanuel had told him in detail how to get to the hive and when Joseph first read the words, he had piloted an Apache Attack helicopter behind the bees to the baobab tree.

✿   ✿   ✿

"If plants and insects and birds could speak, and if we listened, they would tell us hundreds of stories about how changes in our climate are affecting life all over the world."

Daisy's father was walking with his old familiar quick, lengthy, confident stride inspecting the almond fruit forming on their trees. The harvest wasn't bad and Bill Campbell was getting new bees from Australia for next spring. Daisy skipped to keep up with him.

"We've got to start listening more. Things're always changing. We'll adapt. Cut down on pesticides and herbicides; find alternatives; breed new types of bees. You know, they reckon every third bite of food we eat depends on those little creatures. It may take a while but we'll crack it. We have to."

✿　✿　✿

Rescuers had found a cold, wet and hungry Emmanuel. Joseph's directions were precise. Emmanuel had not found much honey that time, but what he had, he put in a jar. A month later, when Chilabula village was coming back to life, Emmanuel and his family sent the honey to Joseph as a thank you. It was the best Joseph had ever tasted.

Tommo and the Bike Train

by Miriam Halahmy

As a teacher in Camden we studied floods in Bangladesh. People lost everything and that wasn't the worst cruelty. Worldwide flooding will increase with global warming. In my story, inspired by those lessons, Tommo is a Camden schoolboy, suddenly whisked away to live by the sea. Terrible floods are coming, threatening Granny Marble next door, who is too old to run away. What will happen to all the grannies in the world if the sea levels rise? Tommo decides to stop climate change in his neighbourhood personally. Perhaps it will give you some ideas of what to do.

"Frigging Biggin!" shouted Tommo to a passing seagull.

There was no one to call him mad. The beach was completely empty. No buses, no tube trains, no kebab shops, no mates, no street lights. Biggin-on-Sea almost had no pavements!

Deep would laugh like a drain if he could see this dump!

Deep was his best mate. His real name was Deepak and his parents were from Bangladesh.

He and Deep had just been chosen for the Year 7 football team, when Tommo's parents announced they were moving to Suffolk on the east coast of England.

"Out of London?" said Tommo, his voice rising in disbelief when they told him.

"Your dad's got a new job, caretaker in a school by the sea," said his mum. "We love the seaside, don't we?"

"Not to live," said Tommo, stunned. "Camden's my home, I ain't going nowhere."

Dad shook his head slowly, running a hand through his shock of red hair. "London's gone rotten, Tommo. Gangs, stabbings, muggings..."

"Gridlocked roads, pollution," added his mum.

"Pollution!" yelled Tommo angrily. "I don't need clean air, and me and Deep know all the gangs. We keep well clear."

"We're moving in two weeks," snapped Dad.

By the end of October, Tommo found himself stuck in a stone cottage at the end of a lane. There were no proper neighbours; just an old woman, who lived a few metres away and muttered to herself all day. The wind howled continuously on the flat, grey beach and the sea was like a ferocious dog off its lead.

On the first school morning a mobile phone appeared on his breakfast plate. "What's this for?" he said.

"In case you get lost, love," replied his mother.

"What, in Frigging Biggin?" said Tommo, scornfully.

But Deep had a phone. His dad sold mobiles, so he was always on the best network. He sent Deep a text as Dad drove him to school.

Big sucks wots up T

Deep rang him back.

"All right, mate?" came Deep's cheery, familiar voice.

"Nothing to do here," moaned Tommo. "It's so boring."

"Sorry mate," said Deep vaguely. "Find out about the football team. Gotta go now and meet Dax for school."

Disappointed, Tommo said goodbye and stared gloomily out of the car window at the huge empty fields.

By the end of the week Tommo thought he would go insane. It was already November and dark before he got home. Outside the windows of the cottage nothing moved, except the wind and the sea.

In London, he thought miserably, everyone would be getting ready for Bonfire Night. He missed playing football under the street lights, the neon sign of Ozman Kebabs flashing in the winter gloom.

After dinner, while his parents watched TV, he texted Deep.

Goin mad. Wots up. T

Deep rang him. "Dax got your place on the team."

"What, that meathead? He's a disaster zone!" *I've been replaced*, thought Tommo. *Am I a Camden boy any more*? "Deep, mate, I can't stand it here. Come over, can't you?"

"Mate, how can I? Anyway, Auntie Mina is coming to stay from Bangladesh. Mum says I'm not allowed nowhere."

"School's rubbish," said Tommo, miserably.

"The football team is full of fat nerds."

Tommo had asked Jeremy, a podgy boy in his form, if they needed a striker. "I'm good, Jez, mate."

"Actually, I prefer Jeremy and the team's full. I play defence."

Tommo had stared at the other boy in astonishment as he adjusted his glasses. He only reached to Tommo's collar.

"There's no tuck shop," Tommo moaned, as Deep snickered down the phone, "no chips at school dinner, they've gone all healthy and Geography sucks."

Geography had always been Tommo's favourite subject; he kept a map on his bedroom wall and marked all the places round the world where England played matches. But nothing felt the same in his new school.

"All we do is pollution, pollution, pollution. The teacher's mad. Honest! He thinks they should melt down all the cars in Britain. Then yesterday he started on about global warming and Bangladesh."

"Cool," said Deep with interest. "Where's he from?"

"Frigging Biggin," snorted Tommo. "But he says Bangladesh is always flooding, and cars make the planet hotter, which makes the sea levels rise and Bangladesh is gonna sink," laughed Tommo. "I yelled out, 'Rubbish!'" he finished proudly.

Tommo had tried to explain that he knew all about Bangladesh. "My mate Deep comes from there," he had said, glaring round the class. "And he never said anything about no floods." But everyone just laughed at his London accent. Tommo had gone bright red and slumped back in his chair. That was the problem with Scottish genes. White skin, red hair, cheeks that let you down in a nanosecond.

But to his amazement, Deep said, "Your teacher's right."

"You what?" said Tommo, confused.

"My dad says Bangladesh has always had floods. Usually everyone just copes with it.

But it's getting much worse because the planet's heating up. He wants Auntie Mina to come to live with us."

"You never said nothing about no flooding!"

"Not exactly Premier League news is it?" said Deep. "Last year when they had floods my grandma died."

"Drowned?" asked Tommo, shocked.

"Snake bite."

There was a silence and then Deep said, "When there's a flood, people escape on to the roofs. But the snakes also creep up there, they've got nowhere else left to go and they kill dozens of people. There's lots of horrible ways to die in a flood."

✿   ✿   ✿

Tommo couldn't sleep that night, imagining snakes under the bed. He almost got up to check.

In IT the next day he googled, *Bangladesh, Floods, DEATH.* He couldn't believe it; people died from drowning, lightning, diseases, collapsed buildings and snake bites!

"Going on your holidays?" asked Jeremy, leaning over with interest.

Tommo just glared at him.

The more he read, the more he felt his skin crawl. *If the earth gets hotter and the sea levels rise,* he thought, *all the snakes in Bangladesh will be sneaking about looking for new homes.* Millions of people will get bitten. Deep's grandma hadn't stood a chance. No wonder they wanted Auntie Mina to move to England, she had a two year old.

✧ ✧ ✧

At the weekend his mum and dad were still busy unpacking. *Another rubbish day on the beach,* thought Tommo, and took his bike from the shed. The sky was grey but at least it wasn't raining. *I should be playing football with Deep*, he thought angrily, thudding the front wheel against a fence post.

I could go over to Jeremy's, he thought reluctantly, then he remembered there was a school match.

"Come and watch," Jeremy had said, cheerfully.

I'd rather bang nails in my feet, thought Tommo.

"Don't just stand there, boy. Bring in the milk!"

Tommo was startled by the voice of the old woman from the next cottage. She was standing in her front garden, wearing a red fleece, dark trousers and rubber ankle boots. A marmalade cat was weaving in and out of her legs. Short grey hair stood up at odd angles on her head and as she turned round and went into the cottage, Tommo could see she had a hump on her back.

For a second he thought of witches.

"Tea and cake, tea and cake, don't be late," came the woman's reedy voice and he heard a strange whistling sound behind her.

A bottle of milk stood on a brick just outside the garden gate. *Might as well*, thought Tommo, suddenly curious. He picked up the milk and walked up the path to the cottage.

The front door opened straight into the downstairs room which was a kitchen and living room combined. It was sparsely furnished, with a small wooden table, two upright chairs and an armchair with the stuffing leaking out. An old-fashioned kettle whistled merrily on the stove.

"Bring it here, that's a dear," sang out the old woman and she wrapped a grubby cloth round the handle of the kettle and slowly poured water into a huge brown teapot.

"I'm Granny Marble, lived here sixty-five year. Ain't that marvellous, dear?"

Tommo didn't answer. He couldn't think of

anything marvellous about Frigging Biggin.

"We had floods, 1953, from the North Sea," Granny Marble went on.

"Floods?" Tommo's ears pricked up. *Like Bangladesh?* he thought mystified.

"Lost the lot, all gone to pot," went on Granny Marble. "Next Friday, in time for tea, storm surge in the North Sea. Like in '53. Ain't going nowhere this time," and she shook a teaspoon at Tommo's nose. Her blue eyes glittered. "Past my prime."

Tommo looked round the shabby room. *What a dump*, he thought, *wouldn't matter if it was washed out to sea. Anyway, what does she know about floods, sitting here all day talking to herself in crazy rhymes.*

Then he had a horrible thought.

"What about snakes?" he said.

"Want one of these cakes?" she rhymed, and gave him a sneaky grin.

"No," muttered Tommo irritably. "Were there any snakes in the floods?"

"Snakes in Biggin, what you thinkin'?" and Granny Marble gave a shrill laugh. "When the water comes it covers the beach, right out of reach, covers the huts, covers the road. Float out the door, all gone, no more."

Her voice sank softly and there was the sound of rain, smacking as if in a bad temper, against the windows. Tommo stared into Granny Marble's eyes, shining in the firelight. How deep was the water if everything floated out the door? Three metres, four? Where would all the animals go, the foxes and the rabbits in their deep dark holes?

And the snakes in the long grass by the roadside, whispered a voice in Tommo's head.

☼ ☼ ☼

That night Tommo sat up with his parents watching the news.

"Not like you, love. Doing something in school?" said his mum, as she put biscuits out on a plate.

"Climate change," muttered Tommo, yawning as the Prime Minister droned on about terrorists. Then the weatherman came on and suddenly there was a close up of the east coast of England.

"There's Suffolk," said Dad frowning. "Right where we are."

The weatherman said that a storm surge was due down the North Sea at the end of the week. *Granny Marble was right*, thought Tommo, amazed. *Maybe she* is *a witch*.

"The sea level could rise by three metres," said the weatherman.

"Just like in 1953," said Dad. "Hundreds died on these coasts."

"And is it all because of global warming?" asked Tommo.

"Well, if the sea levels rise things will only get worse round here," nodded Dad.

"I'll get in some extra tins," said Mum anxiously.

"Granny Marble's cottage was flooded last time," said Tommo. *Should I warn Dad about the snakes?* he thought with a shiver. *We could get a gun or a knife.*

Picturing weapons in sleepy Biggin made him laugh out loud.

"What's funny, love?" asked Mum.

"You thought it would be safer here. I don't think Deep's gonna drown in Camden!"

☼   ☼   ☼

But it wasn't funny really. In assembly on Thursday morning the Head said, "School's closed for the rest of the week. We could all be flooded and many of you will have to leave your homes."

"We'll have to cancel the match on Saturday,"

whispered Jeremy in a worried voice.

That's all they care about, thought Tommo, *playing football and keeping their iPods dry.*

But what about the snakes?

"We'll be an evacuation centre," said the Head, "so some of you will be sleeping here. Go home and do everything your parents tell you. Biggin could be under water tomorrow night."

By Friday morning it was raining hard. Tommo pulled back his bedroom curtains and looked out at the sea. Was he imagining it or was it already halfway up the beach? His parents had decided to evacuate the cottage after lunch and they spent the morning loading the car and fixing locks to the doors and windows.

"You get looters in floods," said Dad grimly.

Tommo added looting to his list of flood dangers.

But secretly he had already decided that the cottage would get completely washed away, the school would collapse and Mum and Dad would move back to London. No snakes there, except in the zoo and he'd be back in the football team before Christmas. *Bring on the floods!*

By two o'clock the car was loaded to the brim and they set off down the lane. Tommo craned his neck to see if he could spot Granny Marble.

"Did they come and get her?" he asked Mum.

"Oh yes," said Mum, looking anxiously at the heavy rain lashing the windscreen. "They'd get the old people first."

But Tommo wasn't so sure. "Did you actually see her go?" he cried out, above the screaming of the wind. There was a quick movement on the road and he jumped in his seat. *A snake?* he wondered.

"I'm sure she's gone, love. We'll see her at the school."

The car crunched over something solid in the road and Dad slammed on the brakes.

"Damn!" he yelled. "Blown a tyre. I'll have to change it."

As Dad went round to the back of the car, Tommo made up his mind.

Wrenching open the door against the gale, he cried out, "Won't be a minute."

Before Mum could stop him, he was running down the road, parka hood blown back, freezing rain drenching his head. His trainers were soaked as he reached the garden gate. Tommo hesitated and glanced towards the beach. What if the sea came roaring in now and washed them away? It felt like a wild beast, lurking untamed beyond the flimsy cottages. Should he make a run for it while he could?

I have to be sure, Tommo decided, *even if there are snakes*!

He ran up to the front door. It was ajar and no light showed in the room beyond.

"Granny Marble, are you there?"

No sound, not even the mewing of the cat. He reached for a light switch, found one by the door and pressed it. Nothing.

The power must be down, he thought,

but he could see a small shape humped in the armchair in front of the dying embers of the fire. *Run, now!* he told himself, but his feet were glued to the spot.

Then his phone rang. It was Deep. "Mate, hope you're somewhere nice and dry."

"Deep, she's not moving," cried out Tommo in a panic. "I don't know what to do!"

"What?" said Deep. "Who's not moving? Where are you?"

"Granny Marble, she's sort of lying in her chair and her hand's freezing cold. I'm in her cottage."

"You're insane! Tommo, mate, you gotta get out of there, you gotta run, the floods are coming and Auntie Mina says you can't out-run the water. She was in the floods with Granny in Bangladesh, she had her baby in her arms and Granny couldn't run to the boats. She got left behind. Auntie Mina cries all the time. You got to go!

NOW Tommo, RUN! –"

The phone went dead and then a voice shouted his name. It was Dad. Grabbing him round the shoulders, as Tommo sobbed and sobbed, Dad dragged him back to the car and drove as fast as he could to the school.

You can't out-run the water, swept round and round Tommo's head. He had left Granny Marble and now the snakes would eat her dead body.

At the school, Tommo zipped himself into his sleeping bag and pulled his hood over his head. He didn't want to speak to anyone. Mum offered him a jam sandwich but he just burrowed deeper into his parka.

Jeremy came over and prodded him. "The sea's right over the beach huts. Wanna play Scrabble?"

Tommo, already drifting into sleep, didn't answer. As he dozed fitfully, on and off, all he could think about was, *Frigging climate change*.

Dad had said Granny Marble probably had a heart attack, but what about all the other grannies in England and Bangladesh and all around the world?

The earth was getting hotter and the sea levels were rising.

Grannies can't out-run the floods!

They're all going to die, he thought desperately, *from drowning, poisoning in dirty water and snake bites.*

Millions of grannies were doomed unless they did something quickly!

It took all night for the room to finally quieten down and then, just before dawn, when the only sound was snoring, his brilliant plan came to him. All he needed to do was collect mobile numbers from all the kids before they went home.

He persuaded Jeremy to help. "Can't see what for," he grumbled, packing away his Scrabble set.

But Tommo insisted. "Trust me; I know what I'm doing. I'm from Camden."

School didn't open again until the following Wednesday. In the end there hadn't been much flooding but Tommo had decided there was no time to spare. His plan was to stop heating up the earth over Biggin-on-sea and make the other kids see that they could fight climate change. He sent out a text which began, *Save Biggin grannies!*

At eight o'clock on Wednesday morning Tommo set off on his bike. At the top of the lane, Jeremy and two other kids from school were waiting for him.

"All right, mate?" called Jeremy, cleaning his glasses on a grubby cloth. Tommo gave a big grin.

"Let's roll!" he said and the little procession set off along the road.

At all the cottages, outlying farms and villages they collected more and more cyclists, until almost forty kids from Year 7 to the Sixth Form had joined them, laughing and chatting as they went.

As they arrived at school they heard the Headmaster boom out in his Sergeant Major voice, "What's all this?"

"Tommo's Bike Train," cried the cyclists.

"You what?" said the Head, arms folded.

"Better than being driven to school, isn't it sir? Less cars on the road," said Jeremy. "Cycling helps stop climate change and it's safer if we all bike together, like in a train."

"Hummph," said the Head. "Whose idea was this?" and he glared around at the gathering crowd.

"Mine," said Tommo. He felt his cheeks flame brighter than Granny Marble's fire. "Grannies can't out-run floods," he explained. "In Bangladesh they have to go on the roofs, but then the snakes find them and kill them. We want to stop worse floods happening."

"Yes, well," boomed the Head. "Just this once then, but we can't have all these bikes in school every day."

Tommo's heart sank and a groan went up round the playground.

But then the Head said, "I suppose we could

discuss it at the next Governors' meeting."

There's still a chance, thought Tommo and he started to push his bike to the sheds. But his path was blocked by three sets of wheels. Puzzled, he looked up to see Jeremy and two other boys from his class.

"Maybe we could use another striker on the football team," grinned Jeremy. "All right to practice after school?"

Tommo stared at them for a few seconds. Then he gave a brief nod.

But inside a great big *YEEESSSSS!!* bubbled up.

He couldn't wait to text Deep.

Climate [Short] Change

by Lily Hyde

Siberia is so vast, so wild, that it's hard to believe anything we do could affect it. In fact, global warming is completely altering its landscapes, and therefore the way of life of its native people. Modern transport and communications – major contributors to climate change – have brought together communities from around the globe, like the Siberian villagers and West European scientists who meet in this story. But to make a positive difference to our world, we have to be willing to understand not only the abstract causes and effects of climate change, but also each other's daily lives, hopes and dreams.

Climate change is what is happening to the world today. It is turning our Siberian tundra into lakes and then the lakes dry up and in the end we will have no way to live any more. It is people with factories and technology who are causing climate change.

In our village we got to know about climate change this summer when a scientific research expedition from Germany, France and Britain arrived. In Europe people really care about climate change. I will give you a funny example of how much they care: the scientists had an FSB escort driving out of Noyabrsk who wouldn't let them stop near the oil and gas fields. They are State Secrets but Professor Helpmann wanted to collect soil samples so he told the scientists to say they needed to pee. Ben said "We kept drinking and stopping to pee and drinking and peeing, but then we ran out of water and those security service goons got suspicious so next time Dad wanted to stop he stuck his fingers down his

throat and made himself puke. Three times."
Ben's dad is Professor Helpmann. He is mad.

Ben's my age. He's half-German-half-English but he speaks Russian because Professor Helpmann takes him on loads of expeditions to Siberia and at home they have a Russian housekeeper. I'm half-Nenets-half-Russian but my dad never takes me anywhere except into the tundra with the reindeer or the fishing nets, and our only housekeeper is my mum and sister. There's not much of our house to keep anyway. Ben says this is good because it's better for the planet if you live simply and don't have freezers and washing machines and things. If everyone lived like us climate change would never have happened. Mum always complains because she wants a flat in town with running water and heating so I never thought there was anything good about our house. That's why I like Ben. He makes me think things I never thought before.

We brought Ben back to the village with us.

We were in town selling fish and the FSB people had left the expedition there because there are no State Secrets further on, just lakes and reindeer and villages like ours. The scientists were waiting for transport but the Professor didn't want to wait. So we took him and Ben. It is a nine-hour trip through bogs in our ancient UAZ jeep which broke down like it always does. And then they stayed in our house. Mum was embarrassed. Our house is so small Professor Helpmann fills up most of it.

When the other scientists arrived Professor Helpmann held a meeting and everyone went. Most of us had never seen foreigners before. I've never seen many people at all really. In our village the reindeer outnumber the people by about ten to one. The meeting was supposed to tell us about climate change and why the scientists had come but it was hard to understand because the translator from Noyabrsk didn't know half the technical words, and so Professor Helpmann started talking Russian himself but he made lots of mistakes. For example:

Translator: Methane is, er, a gas from a conservatory or hothouse. If it is released from our Siberian bogs as the permafrost melts without, er, going rusty, the result will be a disastrous acceleration in, um, heating up the sphere.

Us: ??????????

Prof. Helpmann: No, no! Methane he GREENHOUSE gas! Now that permafrost she– she– she as ice-cream in sun, if methane he not OXIDISED then will go faster GLOBAL WARMING!

Us: ????????!!!!!!!!!!!!!!

Ben (in my ear): I'll explain after. Stop laughing.

I wasn't the only one laughing but a bit later everyone sat up because the translator and

Prof. Helpmann said something much more interesting:

Translator: We scientists will be here for only a few months. But we want to support you in Siberia to take responsibility for understanding the climate alteration that affects your lives every day. To that end we will give you small, er, gratuities, to set up, er, checking projects.

Us: ???? Gratuities?????

Prof. Helpmann: No, no! We give you GRANTS in THREE THOUSAND EUROS to MONITOR the CLIMATE CHANGE after we go, because climate change he HERE in your front door!

Us: !!!!!!!!!!!!!!!!!!????? MONEY!!

There is not much money in our village.

"Tell us about the grants," I said to Ben afterwards and so did Uncle Vasya and my cousins and most of the neighbours. But Ben was quite cross he wanted to explain climate change and gases like methane warming up the atmosphere. This is especially important here in Siberia because it is causing the permafrost to melt and this releases lots more methane, in fact Siberian bogs contain a quarter of all the methane stored on land in the world. If it is released without being converted into carbon dioxide it will really speed up climate change.

"So what?" said Dad. He is worried about fish and never thinks about anything else. "Tell us about the grants."

"But don't you understand how important it is?" Ben said. "Look, you must have noticed how there are more lakes here than there used to be. That's climate change. I told you global warming is causing the permafrost in the ground to melt. This forms lakes, and at first the lakes get bigger, but after a while they'll disappear again because when the ground melts all through the water just drains away." Ben looked round at us.

"The lakes are the visible part of climate change. Now do you get it?"

Yes we got it, and this is why: if I was going to start this all over again I would write not about foreign scientists or methane gas but about my dad. Dad used to be a reindeer herder. At first he worked for the government collective farm but then that collapsed so Dad started up on his own. Everyone laughed because he had just three reindeer to start with, then four, then seven, then he went into partnership with Uncle Vasya and together they had sixteen reindeer. I know this is still not very many but it was enough not just for us but to sell the meat and fur and antlers, so we got a TV and my sister Zhanna went to study at the school in town. And the reindeer had more calves and one summer we had twenty-two reindeer.

But that was when the lakes started getting bigger. I mean they had been getting bigger for a while. Even whole new ones kept appearing. But that summer there was just too much lake and not enough grazing ground any more. People starting arguing over which ground belonged to what herd, and because our herd was the smallest we lost the arguments. Dad and Uncle Vasya had to go further than they'd ever been for pasture and they got to a place where there were wolves and lost eight reindeer.

Dad says the herd stopped trusting him after that. He says there's a kind of pact between reindeer and herder. They're not like cows or pigs – reindeer are not domestic. They are wild really. They are like proud delicate children, you have to win their trust. After that summer some of our reindeer went back to being properly wild and ran away, and the rest got sick and they died.

The herd lost heart, Dad says. But I think really he lost heart and found the bottle instead. But he got his heart back again eventually. He said "If the Earth so much doesn't want me to be a reindeer herder that its lakes have swallowed up our grazing grounds, then the Earth must want me to be a fisherman instead."

And he started fishing in Blue Lake. He got a big net, then three nets, then he went into partnership again with Uncle Vasya and they got new fish stock and put them in the lake and had ten nets. No one else was selling that kind of fish so two summers later we didn't just buy back the old telly we got a new big one.

But that was when Blue Lake started shrinking again. And some of the new lakes that had appeared got smaller or vanished. Dad and Uncle Vasya tried to move the stock to Green Lake but it is further away and lots of the fish went bad by the time Dad gets them to town. We don't have anywhere to store them. Dad is always saying we need a freezer but we can't afford one. The summer the foreigners came Dad was starting to lose heart all over again, and find the bottle.

So now you will get it why Uncle Vasya said again to Ben that evening, "NOW tell us about the grants."

And Ben did. The scientists were going to

stay for the summer collecting peat samples to see what was in it and how much the permafrost was melting, and mapping the lakes and how much bigger or smaller they were getting, and testing the soil and the air and the moss and everything. Then they'd go back to Europe and analyse all the results. But because climate change doesn't stop when foreigners stop researching they wanted us to carry on testing and checking and mapping, and give us money from the European Union for it.

It seemed so easy. My sister wrote a grant proposal, like a plan to show exactly how we would work and spend the money on equipment for monitoring there were strict rules about that. My sister is the only clever one in our family, but Thierry one of the scientists helped. He is a student from France and he really likes Zhanna because she is pretty. Actually they weren't just working on the proposal together but we didn't know that then. I went on expeditions with Ben and the others to learn about the practicalities of monitoring climate change. It was cool. There was a machine that drills out core samples like cloudy half-frozen sausages from the ground. I learned how to survey with a theodolite and with satellites with GPS or Global Positioning System and Ben has got the greatest knife with loads of blades he let me use. He said he'd give it to me when he left. But what I liked best was Ben telling me funny things about Germany and me telling him about Siberia. And I liked the mosquitoes. I mean I didn't really like them but the foreigners hated them and that was great, I learned loads of swear words in three languages.

We got a grant! We had to register as a non-profit organisation first and be official but that takes ages and Prof. Helpmann is so impatient he put the first part of the money into a bank account Mum opened in town. Our organisation was my family and Uncle Vasya's. Two other families in our village got grants too. We called our organisation 'Hope from Climate Change'.

It was my sister's idea.

It turned out my sister was hoping for a lot from climate change. She finally told us what she had been doing with Thierry. She had applied to study ecology on a special course in France.

"You can't speak French, silly," I said.

"Don't be daft; we can't pay for you to study in France," Mum said.

And Dad said, "We need you here."

My sister went all pale and desperate. All she wants is to go to college but the nearest in Tomsk is too far away and we don't have any money.

"It's a special course for people from all over the world," Zhanna said. "They have lots of students from Russia, and if you're from a poor country directly affected by climate change they will pay for everything. Thierry says I'm sure to get a free place." She said 'Thierry says' quite a bit more before she shouted "but you've got the grant now so you don't need me here anymore!" and ran outside to sulk.

"Don't worry," Mum said. "She won't get

a place. Why should they want a half-wild native Siberian in France?"

But Dad was angry. It's strange how the foreign scientists took over our village. Most of us liked them. We started doing new things and thinking new thoughts, but my dad didn't like them. He started liking the bottle more. At first Prof. Helpmann had talked to him. He went to visit the reindeer herders but he said afterwards there were too many reindeer and it was not ecologically sustainable, and he went to visit Dad and Uncle Vasya at Green Lake but he said their new fish stock was disrupting the natural eco-balance of the lake. At first I thought Prof. Helpmann was interested in everything but now I think he is only interested in one thing and that is climate change and that is why he is mad. I realised this when the disaster at Green Lake happened.

With Zhanna working on the grant and me learning how to monitor climate change, even Mum got a job cooking for the foreigners, there was no one to help smoke or dry or pickle the fish from Green Lake to preserve them. I told you we haven't got a freezer to store fresh fish and so they go bad before Dad can get them to town to sell. He and Uncle Vasya kept them in a pit dug down into the permafrost near Green Lake. But we are experts in climate change now. We know that the permafrost is melting and it is a big problem for global warming. Our fish store melted and flooded and all the fish went rotten.

Mum and Zhanna had gone to town with some of the scientists to look at the equipment we have to buy for the monitoring project. We need a computer and a modem and printer. I was really excited about the computer. I thought it would look funny in our house. But when Zhanna got back she was excited about something else. She said "I got a place at the college in France. They will pay for the course and for living expenses and Thierry says all the researchers will club together to help with my air fare."

And Dad said "Curse your college in France. We're finished. We'll all have to work our fingers off preserving the fish however we can. You can't leave."

Zhanna shouted "I've got to go, I'll never get another chance! You can't stop me and anyway you've got the grant now, you've got money–"

Dad slapped her. "You shut up, my girl! What grant? *!!!!!**@!! computers and *****!!@! modems won't feed and clothe my two children and Vasya's four. Curses on all foreign scientists and colleges. They can go to hell."

Zhanna burst into tears and then Mum said "Shut up both of you and listen to me. We haven't bought the computer or anything yet, and in town that wasn't all I looked at."

✿   ✿   ✿

When Prof. Helpmann came to visit us the last time he was a disappointed man. He always was too big for our house but now he could only just squeeze inside with Ben because almost all the space was filled by the freezer. It hums and buzzes. Prof. Helpmann looked at it like it had done him an injury.

He said (or Ben said because he translated when his father got stuck) "This is a gross misuse of our money and our trust."

Dad offered Prof. Helpmann a drink.

"No thank you," Prof. H said. "You know the grant was for a climate change project. Your proposal listed how you were going to spend every penny of it. Nowhere did it list a freezer and if it had done you wouldn't have got the money."

"!!!*****@! climate change," said Dad.

"You didn't say that in your proposal either," Prof. H said. He got rather red. "I thought you understood that climate change affects ALL OF US. If you care about the future, about your children, you must realise that NOTHING matters more than climate change. We wanted to involve you in our work because even though the cause may seem far away the results are right here, with you, in Siberia."

"And how are my children supposed to live while we are messing around testing this and mapping that and fiddling with computers and GSP?" Dad asked.

"It's GPS not GSP," I whispered and he belted me.

"We're scientists, not humanitarian aid workers," Prof. H said. "It's not our job to hand out charity. Maybe I wish we could, but we can't. We wanted to build up a relationship of mutual respect and trust. Together we could have done great things towards saving the planet, if you'd only been able to look beyond your own backyard."

Dad sat up then and said something good. He does that sometimes. I was proud of him even if he had just belted me.

"In this backyard I do what my ancestors did – herd reindeer and catch fish," he said. "My people, the Nenets, made a pact with the Earth that we kept for hundreds of years while you in Europe were ruining it with your factories and technology. And now you come here and think you can tell us how to live and give us money to look at the mess you made. You don't know anything about trust."

Then Dad spoiled it by saying a lot of very rude things and knocking over the bottle. It broke. Prof. Helpmann was not impressed.

"I can't take the freezer away from you, or demand the money back. We'll just have to chalk this one up to experience. But we won't give you any more money, and unfortunately we won't be continuing any projects in this area in future. I'm sorry," he said.

Dad told him to leave or he would throw him out but before Prof. Helpmann went he lifted the lid of the freezer and peeked inside at all the packed fish. He never can resist investigating everything. It made me think of him putting his fingers down his throat to puke. "I said you were destroying the lake's eco-system with these fish," was the last thing he said. "And I'll tell you something else for nothing: if you keep catching them at this rate you'll overfish and there won't be any stock at all next year."

And Ben said to me sadly "You could at least have bought a newer model. These old freezers release so many CFCs they ruin the ozone layer. In most of the world they've been banned."

Soon after that the scientists packed up to leave. Me and Ben said goodbye. At first Ben said "See you next summer," but I said nothing and Ben got a bit red. "Well, Siberia is really huge you know, and we'll probably go to a different part of it next year. If you'd got the computer and modem for the project we could have e-mailed each other at least." Then he said "Maybe I'll see you in Germany or France, you might come and visit your sister."

"I won't," I said. Zhanna is getting ready

to go to college in France. She is working on an essay they've given her to write before she starts. She is so happy, it's not fair.

I wanted to tell Ben I was glad I'd met him and we never would have met if it wasn't for climate change. But I didn't and Ben didn't say anything like that either but he did give me his knife like he promised. I used it to sharpen a pencil so I could write this. The essay Zhanna has got to write is about climate change in her community. She asked me if I had any ideas and I said no I didn't want to help her with her !!****!!@! essay. But then I started thinking and I couldn't stop, I don't know why. I don't suppose it's what those professors are interested in but here it is: my essay about climate change and how it changed my family.

Moonlight

by Karen Ball

This story is set in Sri Lanka – a country where climate change is making the summers hotter and this is leading to an increase in the spread of deadly malaria. I pictured the sloping, green hills and a girl who might work on one of the country's tea plantations. I made her the breadwinner of the family, because all over the world children are forced to grow up quickly. I haven't visited Sri Lanka, but I enjoyed researching details for the story – what would the children eat, what plants and flowers would surround them, which games would they play? A little bit of research and a strong imagination can go a long way...

My name is Chandrika. I was born during the night in the single room my parents shared. I was named after the silver light that blessed my birth – it means *moonlight*. My parents no longer live on the plantation; they died when I was young. I remember my mother's eyes and the gold bracelets that jangled on her wrists. That is all. I take care of my family now; I am all my younger brothers have.

That morning I woke at dawn, just as I had for as many dawns as I could remember. The mists hung low over the emerald hills and I wrapped my cotton shawl tightly around my shoulders. The earth felt fresh beneath my toes and my heart squeezed tight with happiness as I gazed down on the slopes. I live in a very beautiful place; I don't need a teacher to tell me that. I had to leave school to work in the tea plantation when I was fourteen. I don't mind. While I have two hands to dance over the tea plants and fill my basket with green leaves, what use do I have for a pen and paper? The alphabet won't fill my brothers' stomachs.

I went to the shared water tap with my kettle. It is one of the few items my brothers and I own and every morning I give thanks for its battered sides. Without its cheerful whistle, how would I get my brothers out of their beds? I filled the kettle and then I plunged my hands under the cool water, bringing them up to wash my face. The water felt good against my skin. I could already sense the heat of the day creeping up behind me. I gazed back down at the hills and saw that the dawn mist was burning off. The ghostly swirls seemed to disappear earlier and earlier each day – it had been a hot summer.

I walked back to our line room. It is only small, but so are all the rooms on the estate. No one complains; we know we are lucky to be working and to have a shelter over our heads. I could feel my heavy plait swinging behind my back as I walked past all the other families.

"Good morning!" Amanthi called out, grinning. She is our neighbour. She wears a beautiful gold stud in her nose and her coffee-coloured skin always glows golden in the morning sunshine. I cannot help but smile every time I see her.

"Good morning, Amanthi," I called back. "Did you have good dreams last night?" She burst out laughing and shook her head at me. Everyone knows Amanthi always dreams of fudge made from palm treacle.

I heaved the kettle on to its stand above the fire. As I waited for it to boil, I sat on my haunches and made breakfast for the boys, patting out rice-flour pancakes that I grilled over the fire. The aroma of the pancakes drifted under Babiya and Nimal's nostrils and I watched to see whose eyelashes would flutter open first. I would never tell the boys this, but they both have beautiful eyelashes. Long and thick – the type my girlfriends would love to have. I know, because they tell me.

Nimal was the first to stretch his arms above his head.

"Is that breakfast I can smell?" he asked. I watched him climb out of bed and wander over, rubbing the sleep from his eyes. He reached out and picked a pancake off the toasting fork, batting it from hand to hand as he waited for it to cool down. He didn't wait long enough. "Chandrika," he protested, as he burnt his tongue, "do you have to make the pancakes so hot?"

I thrust the toasting fork into his hand and pretended to bat him round the head as I jumped to my feet.

"Don't be so cheeky," I said, walking to the door. "And make sure Babiya is up and ready for school. I'll see you this evening." Nimal grunted in answer; I knew that was all the conversation he was capable of this early in the morning.

Amanthi was waiting for me outside our room. Together, we walked down to the plantation. The green, sloping hills fell below us. At their base was a smooth lake, its waters reflecting the cloud-covered sky.

We picked up our baskets and tied them to each other's backs. They were big – big enough to hold a whole day's pickings. When the sun descended at the end of the day, my back would be aching from the weight of it.

Along with the other girls and women, we walked out on to the terraced slopes. The women's brightly-coloured sashes and their hands, plucking and snipping, made the fields look as though they were being teased by giant butterflies. I reached out to the nearest tea plant, and snapped off two leaves, throwing them over my shoulder into the basket on my back. The first of many.

I know it is wrong to be proud, but I cannot deny the truth: I am a good tea picker. I am always careful to only nip off the two bright green leaves and the berry at the top of each tea plant. You could never make a bitter cup of tea from the leaves that I pluck. I sometimes think about all the people around the world, drinking my tea. It makes me feel very small and humble.

"Are you still saving for university?" Amanthi asked, as we worked side-by-side. I could see that the bottom of her basket was already hidden beneath emerald leaves. I made a silent promise to myself to work faster.

"A few rupees a month," I admitted. "I would love for my brothers to graduate one day. Do you think that can be possible, Amanthi?"

In my heart, I knew this was an impossible dream. But it was a dream that kept me going as I strode down the endless rows of tea. It was better than dreaming of fudge!

"All things are possible," Amanthi said. "You are a determined young woman. You could make anything happen." I felt my face blush at this compliment and put up a hand to wipe away the sheen of sweat that was already covering my cheeks. I batted my hands in front of my face.

"The heat!" I complained. This year was like no other. We had started to call it Agni's Year, after the Hindu god of fire. "It isn't good for the tea." The plants enjoyed the humidity, it was true. But this much heat – with the morning mists disappearing so quickly – made the plants dry and brittle. It was getting more and more difficult to find fresh, juicy tea leaves. And that meant fewer rupees at the end of each day.

As I turned back to my work, a mosquito came to hover in front of my face. Most of the time they only bothered us at sunset, but this summer there were so many that they even hovered in the air on cloudy days. Fortunately, I know what the trick is with mosquitoes – you ignore them. They get so annoyed that they have to fly away and bother someone else. *Go away!* I willed my unwelcome companion. *Leave me alone.*

It was not to be. As I reached up to the cloudy sky to stretch my back, I felt a bite on the tender skin of my inside arm. I snatched my hands back down and rubbed the skin where the mosquito had bitten me. I should have been used to this by now. Sri Lanka is home to many more mosquitoes than it is to girls who work the fields. Especially this summer. But I still hated the cruel bite of these insects.

"Another bite!" I said to Amanthi.

She laughed. "They love you. You must have juicy meat on those young bones."

I couldn't help joining in with her laughter.

It was too beautiful a day.

✿　✿　✿

As I walked back to our line room, tired and hungry, the Golden Shower trees on the boundary of the plantation were heavy with bunches of yellow flowers. The heat had made them blossom in crowds of gold colour, and now their petals lit up the fading sky. They were like candles lighting my way home.

Nimal and Babiya were already home from school and sat, cross-legged, on the dirt floor, playing Pachisi. Babiya threw his cowrie shells on the board to see how many moves he would have next.

"Chandrika!" he cried, as I stepped into the room. "Come and play!" I went to sit down next to them, but as I did so I felt my head become light. I closed my eyes and white dots danced behind my eyelids.

"What is it?" Nimal asked, concerned.

I waved a hand through the air. "It's nothing. I'm tired, that's all," I told him. But Nimal caught hold of my arm and twisted it round so that he could see the pale underside. A large red blush spread out from where the mosquito had bitten me that morning.

"What's this?" he asked. I shrugged my shoulders.

"Another mosquito bite. If I had a rupee for every one of those…" I didn't finish the sentence. We all knew that any joke about precious rupees wasn't funny. Not when our bellies rumbled. "I'll make something to eat. You two, get to your studies."

I watched from the fire as my brothers knelt to their work, spreading out their schoolbooks on the ground. Nimal's brow furrowed in concentration as he worked his way through his sums. He was a clever boy; everyone said so. It gave me a shiver of excitement to think about what he could achieve in life.

As I dished out the broth, the ladle trembled in my hand. I realised that my shiver of excitement had not stopped. And I no longer felt hungry for food. As the boys ate, I crept into bed and pulled the thin sheet over my legs. I prayed that my brothers would not notice how the sheet moved and shifted as my feet jerked beneath it with the racking tremors that now had hold of my body. I turned over in bed and gazed at the mosquito bite. It was angry, red and swollen. I closed my eyes tight shut and prayed. *Please not malaria*, I asked. *Not now. Not yet.* I knew we couldn't afford a doctor even if I could have made the two-day journey to see one. There had been so much malaria this hot summer – more than ever before – that the doctors were overworked. One more girl in the waiting room was the last thing they needed. Besides, there was still so much tea to pick if my dreams were to come true...

I pulled the sheet up to my chin and fell into a fitful sleep.

☼ ☼ ☼

When I woke in the morning, a dull throbbing filled my head. My skin was covered with a sheen of sweat and my joints ached. I could not decide if I felt too hot or too cold and kept pushing the sheets from me, only to hastily gather them around my shoulders the next moment. Light poured into the room and I realised that dawn had long since come and gone.

I had slept in!

"Nimal! Babiya! Why didn't you wake me?"

I called out. But my voice came out thin and weak. Their beds were empty. As I struggled to swing my legs out of the bed, a plump hand pushed me back against the pillow. It was Amanthi.

"You are not going to work today," she said. "The boys are at school. The rest of us have pooled our rupees and called a doctor. He'll be here soon." Despair flooded through me.

"No," I whispered, my mouth dry. I could not afford to stay in bed and my friends could not afford to waste their money on me. I had to get back out to the fields.

I pushed the sheet off me and tried to twist my body out of the bed. But the effort made me wince with pain and I felt nausea rise up through my body. As Amanthi put her arm around my shoulders, I retched. But my stomach was empty.

I looked back up at my friend. "What is happening to me?" I asked.

She could not meet my gaze. At that moment I knew.

"All will be well. Remember, you are a strong young woman." Amanthi's words fell like heavy stones down a well. They disappeared into the darkness of my soul.

I gazed past her at the bright light of the day outside. It made my eyes hurt to look, but I could not turn away. I could see the beautiful greens of the tea plantation. So many greens! Row after row of tea plants. It was all I had ever known and the only picture I had woken up to, day after day. I wouldn't be denied it now.

"Take me outside," I said.

"No, Chandrika," Amanthi protested. "You're too weak."

She was wrong.

"It's all I ask of you," I said. "It's not too much, is it?" I watched as tears brimmed in Amanthi's eyes. You see, I was clever too. I knew how to persuade people. Especially when it was as important as this.

✿　✿　✿

Amanthi and I walked out together. I leant heavily on Amanthi's arm, but she didn't complain. Other families huddled and whispered as they looked at me. I knew what they were thinking. I was thinking the same thing.

Amanthi settled me on a large rock and I gazed out over my homeland. I could see the women working in the fields. I longed to be with them – to feel the glossy wax of the tea leaves beneath my hands; to work for my family. I remembered my mother and wondered if she had ever felt the same way. My vision blurred as shooting pains ran through my limbs. I thought of the family who used to live in Amanthi's room, of the baby who had died from malaria.

A voice sounded out from behind me. When I turned round I saw a tall man carrying a slim leather case. Nimal stood behind him.

"I heard the doctor had been called," he said. "I could not stay in school." I did not have the heart to scold him.

The doctor knelt beside me and reached out a cool palm to feel my forehead. "You should be in bed," he said.

"I know, I tried to –" Amanthi began to say.

"Shush, now," I said. "Sunshine is good for the soul. Even one such as mine."

"There's nothing wrong with your soul," the doctor said. He pulled a syringe and a glass tube out of his bag. "I'd like to take a blood test," he explained. Nimal crept closer and I noticed the way he peered intently at the doctor's equipment.

I held out my arm and the doctor wiped an alcohol-soaked swab of cotton over a patch of skin. Then I looked away and waited. The pain as he drove the needle home was nothing compared to my night sweats. When I turned back, Nimal was watching closely as the doctor filled the sample glass. He pushed a stopper into the glass and passed the test tube to my brother.

"Put this in my case. Carefully," he told my brother. Nimal's face glowed with pride as he carried the test tube over to the battered leather case the doctor had left on the ground. I watched as Nimal held my blood sample up to the sunshine. What clues swirled around in there? I already knew. I had tasted death; I knew its tang. After all, I had buried my mother and father.

"Is it malaria?" Nimal asked, standing back up. His face was solemn now. "We can take the truth." He straightened his shoulders and it broke my heart to watch him being brave.

The doctor turned round to scan the horizon, to gaze down on the tea pickers far below us. I saw the way his hands fisted and the knuckles turned white. He nodded once, grimly.

"Probably," he said. "If only we could do something about this heat. The mosquitoes are worse than ever before." My brother came to stand beside the doctor. The doctor continued to talk, almost to himself. "Of course, people know what is happening – but they prefer to turn their faces away from the truth." Amanthi and

I shared a startled glance. Doctors didn't normally talk in this way. He turned round and strode over to me, lifting my face so that he could peer into my eyes. I tried to keep my gaze steady as the light hurt my eyes.

"You must sleep," he said. His voice broke. "Rest is what you need now." He let go of my chin and my head sank on to my chest. I was exhausted and suddenly I didn't want to be out here any more. I wanted my bed.

As Amanthi helped me back to my room, I heard Nimal ask the doctor questions.

"What can be done?" he asked.

"Things are changing, but slowly," the doctor said. "People must be educated. They must learn to change their ways. Otherwise, the suffering will be even worse."

I paused at my doorway and turned round for one last look. My eyes hungrily ate up the picture of my brother with the doctor's hand resting on his shoulder. Beyond them, the green hills of the tea plantation. My heart filled with hope as I watched the doctor approach me to say goodbye. I could see that his was a kind soul.

"Look after him," I said, gazing up into the man's face. "He has a sharp brain. Help him get to university." The doctor did not look away; he understood. He nodded once. "He has a brother, too," I added.

"They shall have good lives," the doctor said. "And so will their children. If we make the world better. And we *will* make the world better – I promise you that."

"So do I," said Nimal.

I thought of all the people around the world, drinking my tea. Then I turned into the dark of our room. Amanthi shut the door behind us and I climbed stiffly into bed.

✧   ✧   ✧

My name is Chandrika. I died during the night, kissed by the light of the moon, in the room my parents shared. I left behind my brothers – too young to bury a sister. But I also left behind hope. I had seen the fire that burnt in Nimal's heart. He is a clever boy. I know he will do much with his life. I hope he will change the world. As Amanthi said – you never can tell.

All things are possible.

Future Dreaming

by George Ivanoff

Last summer saw some unprecedented extremes of weather in Australia. The state of Victoria, where I live, suffered drought and a heat wave which contributed to devastating bushfires. Meanwhile, the state of Queensland was practically underwater, enduring widespread flooding. Is this a sign of things to come? Climate change is a serious issue. But the future is still unwritten. How climate change will progress is dependent on how we act now. Not just governments, but also ordinary people. Future Dreaming is my attempt to show that the actions of everyone, including kids, are important to the future of our planet.

The storm raged. The water rose, flooding fields, gardens and buildings. The wind howled with tremendous force, sweeping away all that stood in its path. Rain fell from the dark sky in torrential bursts.

Standing in the middle of all this violence was a boy. The wind whipped his wet sandy-coloured hair about his sad face. As he stared pitifully at all the devastation, he silently mouthed a single word: "Help!"

Jade was wet. Her eyes snapped open. She was huddled under her doona, soaked with sweat. It was a cold, crisp morning, but she felt unbearably hot. Kicking off the doona, she closed her eyes again. Images from her dream drifted behind her eyelids. She tried to remember the details of the boy's face. But all she could see was the sadness in his eyes and the single word on his lips.

Jade opened her eyes, suddenly realising that she was cold. She pulled the doona back over herself and shivered. Then she looked over at the clock on her bedside table and yelped. The alarm hadn't gone off. And she was going to be late for school if she didn't get a move on. She threw the doona off again, wrapped her dressing gown around her pyjamas and rushed out of her room to get some breakfast.

"Bit late this morning," said her mother, looking up from her cup of coffee and her copy of the *Financial Review*.

"Forgot to set the alarm," explained Jade as she opened the refrigerator and stuck her head in.

Her mother nodded and sipped at her coffee. "Sleep well?"

Jade emerged with a carton of orange juice. "Um ... not really." She took a swig from the carton.

"Would you please use a glass?" said Jade's mother, shaking her head. "You're thirteen, not three."

Jade took another swig. "I will next time." Then she put the carton back.

"You were calling out in your sleep again last night," said Karen, Jade's older sister.

"You having bad dreams again?" asked their mother.

"Uh-huh," nodded Jade, getting a slice of bread from the freezer and heading for the toaster.

"Well, could you try for quieter dreams tonight," said Karen, yawning and reaching for the jar of instant coffee. "I've got a paper due tomorrow."

"Maybe you should see someone about those nightmares," said their mother, putting down her newspaper.

Jade shifted uncomfortably as she waited for her toast.

"Want a lift to school?" asked Karen, trying the change the subject. "I'm leaving in ten, and I could drive past your school on the way to uni."

"Cool," said Jade, grabbing her toast as it popped up. "I'd better get dressed." She took a huge bite from the piece of dry toast and chucked the rest into the compost container, then headed for her room.

Karen got stuck in the morning peak traffic and Jade was late for school after all. She got a warning from her homeroom teacher and sniggers from her classmates as she tried to sneak into the classroom. As she slumped into her chair, she thought that she would have been better off catching the train.

"And finally this morning," said their teacher, "I'd like to welcome Marc Rider to our school. He and his parents have just moved into the area." The teacher smiled. "Stand up Marc, so the others can see who you are."

A blond-haired boy near the front of the class got tentatively to his feet. He looked around at the staring faces, smiled nervously and quickly sat down again.

"I trust that you will all make Marc feel very welcome," said the teacher. "Now, off to your first class."

As kids started jostling for the door, Jade stared at the new boy – the new boy who looked very familiar.

✿   ✿   ✿

Jade watched the new boy for the rest of the day. She watched him from a distance as he ran around the oval at recess, unsuccessfully trying to join in with the other boys. She stared at the back of his head throughout the day's classes. At lunchtime she sat on one of the benches in the quadrangle, not too far from where he was sitting. She watched him as he ate his sandwich and drank his can of cola. As she watched him, she finally realised that he reminded her of the boy from her dream.

Marc couldn't be the boy from her dream, Jade decided as she ate her own sandwich. It was impossible! Besides, Marc's hair was a little darker, his nose was not quite the same, and he was definitely younger. Still ... he did look an awful lot like the boy in her dream. Much too similar to be a coincidence.

Having finished her sandwich, Jade got the apple out of her lunch box. As she bit into it, she looked up to see Marc bite into his apple and look up. Their eyes met. He smiled and she immediately looked away. When she looked up again, he was walking off, shoulders slumped. As he passed a rubbish bin, he chucked out his empty drink can and the remainder of his apple. Jade watched thoughtfully as he walked away.

When she finished her apple, Jade put the core back into her lunch box. She would take it home and put it into the compost. It was only then that it occurred to Jade that Marc had been eating alone. She wondered where he was from, who his parents were and why he reminded her of the boy in her dream.

"You're a bit weird, aren't you?"

Jade whirled around. Lunchtime was nearly over, but she was still sitting on the bench, alone, lost in thought. Marc must have snuck up behind her.

"Am not!" was all Jade could think of saying in return.

"You've been looking at me strangely all day," said Marc, walking around to the front of the bench. "And now you're just sitting here on your own, staring at nothing. I think that's a bit weird."

"Oh…" replied Jade, realising she couldn't really argue that point. "Sorry! It's just that you … kinda remind me of someone."

"Someone nice, I hope," said Marc, sitting on the bench next to her.

"Don't know," said Jade, looking down at her lunch box, remembering the dream.

"What do you mean you don't know?" asked Marc, puzzled.

"Well … I don't really know the person you remind me of." She didn't look up as she said this.

She realised that what she was saying probably did make her sound rather odd.

"See," said Marc, smirking. "Weird!"

Jade looked up and glared at him. Maybe she was being a bit weird, but she didn't need some misfit new kid telling her so. "Well at least I don't throw cans into the rubbish bin when there's a recycling bin right next to it," she blurted out.

They stared at each other for a few seconds, neither of them knowing what to say next, when the bell, signalling the end of lunchtime, rang. Then suddenly, embarrassed by her outburst, Jade grabbed her lunch box and rushed off without another word.

Marc watched her go and shook his head slowly.

"Weird!"

✿   ✿   ✿

"Help!"

The sandy-haired boy was alone and he was nowhere. There was nothing around him. There was nothing ... anywhere. His hair was matted with sweat. His face was red and damp. His eyes were sad and empty. His lips, cracked and dry. His eyelids started to flutter uncontrollably, and his eyes rolled back, till there was only white. He crumpled, like a puppet whose strings had been cut.

Jade struggled to get to the boy. Something was holding her back, stopping her legs from running, her arms from moving.

A voice from the darkness called, "Jade, are you OK?"

She opened her eyes. Her mother's concerned face looked down at her.

"What?" asked Jade, confused.

"You've had another nightmare," whispered her mother.

"Oh." She propped herself up on an elbow. "Sorry!"

"How about I make you some hot chocolate?" asked her mother, not really knowing what else to do.

Jade nodded with a half-smile. Hot chocolate! It was her mother's solution to everything from skinned knees to family crises, from the death of a pet to ... bad dreams. It meant she had something to do and didn't have to talk about it.

As she got up to follow her mother to the kitchen, Jade shivered, despite being drenched in sweat.

✿   ✿   ✿

Jade waited outside the school counsellor's office, hoping that no one would see her there. Her mother had driven her to school early and was in talking with the counsellor – talking about her; talking about her dreams.

The door finally opened and her mother came out.

"You've got an appointment to see Ms Helmond at lunchtime today."

"Mum, I don't..." began Jade.

"I'd really feel happier if you talked to someone about your dreams," said her mother, cutting her off. "Please!"

Jade looked down at her shoes, sighed, and then nodded. Her mother wasn't a good talker, or listener for that matter, so Jade wasn't really surprised that she was getting her daughter to talk through her problems with a complete stranger.

"Thank you," said her mother. "Now I've got to get to work."

She gave her daughter a quick hug and rushed off. As Jade watched her mother leaving, she noticed Marc walking past. He had a drink can in his hand and a school bag over one shoulder. He stopped by the bins and looked over at her. Then, smiling, he made a big show of dropping the can into the recycle bin rather than the rubbish bin, before continuing on his way.

☼ ☼ ☼

"And you're having these dreams every night?" asked Ms Helmond, the school counsellor, as she shuffled through the papers in Jade's file.

"Pretty much," answered Jade.

Ms Helmond nodded as she continued to look through the file.

"Hmmm," murmured Ms Helmond, head down. "You took part in the school's recycling drive last year." She continued to shuffle through papers. "You wrote a piece for the school magazine on climate change."

Jade nodded as Ms Helmond looked up.

"Environmental issues are really important to you, aren't they Jade?"

Jade nodded again.

"Would you say that climate change and damage to our environment is something that worries you?"

"I guess," answered Jade. "I mean ... I do think about it a bit. You know ... pollution and recycling and stuff."

Ms Helmond nodded thoughtfully. She closed Jade's file and folded her hands together on top of it before looking up at her.

"I think your dreams may simply be manifestations of your anxieties. It's your subconscious telling you that you need to do something to help the world. That's why the boy is asking for help. Maybe, deep down, you're even feeling a little guilty because you're not doing everything that you can."

She smiled. It was a self-satisfied sort of smile that said *I've figured it out, aren't I wonderful.*

"I think you'll find," she continued, "that if you start doing something proactive – saving water, recycling, or whatever – that your subconscious will settle down and the dreams

172

will stop."

She picked up Jade's file, indicating that the session was at an end.

Jade nodded and reached for her school bag.

"So are you nuts?" asked Marc as Jade stepped out of the counsellor's office.

"What are you doing here?" asked Jade, surprised to see him waiting there for her.

"I got lonely eating my lunch with no one staring at me," he smiled, holding up his lunch box.

"Yeah ... funny," said Jade, scowling at him.

"So ... are you?"

"Huh?"

"Are you nuts?"

"No!" said Jade indignantly. "I'm not nuts."

"Then why were you seeing the counsellor?" persisted Marc. "Is it because you keep staring at new kids in a weird kinda way?"

"None of your business," said Jade stalking off. "Get lost!"

"I was just joking," said Marc, following

after her. "I don't really think you're nuts."

Jade continued walking.

"Wanna have lunch together?" he said. "I haven't eaten mine yet."

Jade walked over to the quadrangle, dumped her bag on a bench and slumped down beside it. Marc sat down on the other side of the bag. They both brought out their lunches in silence. Neither of them said anything while they ate. After they were finished, Marc threw his can into the recycle, and then went to put his apple core in the bin.

"I'll take that," said Jade, snatching the core from his hand.

He looked at her strangely.

"Compost," she said, explaining her actions. "We have a compost bin at home."

"Oh," nodded Marc.

"Yeah, I know, that probably makes me even weirder," said Jade.

Then the bell rang and they headed off for class.

✿   ✿   ✿

"So, how did it go?" asked Karen, as Jade walked into the kitchen.

Jade shrugged as she dumped her school bag on the floor by the table. She headed to the refrigerator and got the carton of orange juice.

"Glass," reminded Karen, before Jade had the chance to put the carton to her lips.

Jade nodded and got herself a glass before sitting down at the table, opposite her sister. She filled it up with juice, drained the glass and refilled it.

"Come on," coaxed Karen. "Spill the beans. What did the counsellor say?"

Jade sighed. "She reckons I'm worried about the environment and that I just need to do something positive to make the dreams go away."

"What?"

"She said that my dreams were just

manifestations of my anxieties."

Jade sipped at her juice.

"But that doesn't make sense," complained Karen. "You've been having these dreams, on and off, since you were a little kid. I doubt that you were all that worried about the environment when you were five."

Jade shrugged and drank some more juice.

"What kind of a counsellor is she?" railed Karen. "I mean…"

Karen's voice trailed off as realisation dawned on her. She stared intently at her younger sister. "You didn't tell her the whole story, did you?"

Jade shrugged and stared into her glass of juice.

"Well, what did you tell her?"

"Not much, really," admitted Jade, looking up. "Mum talked to her this morning and told her about my dreams. And I guess she didn't tell her that I used to have them when I was little."

Karen stared at her sister.

"So I guess it's Mum's fault," said Jade,

looking down at her juice again. She suddenly felt guilty about blaming her mother.

"To be fair," said Karen, "Mum probably doesn't even remember you had bad dreams when you were little. She was working an awful lot back then, and I was the one taking care of you."

Karen shook her head and turned to stare out the window. She ran a hand through her short blonde hair and sighed. "OK," she started. "I think there's something I should tell you."

Jade looked up.

"I've had the dreams too," Karen announced. "Not for a long time now. But when I was younger, I had them for a little while. The dreams were always about bad weather – storms and things. And there was someone in them. A kid. I could never really tell if it was a boy or a girl." She looked back at Jade. "They didn't last all that long. I had a few when I was about ten. And then again a couple of years later, when I was your age."

"Wow!" exclaimed Jade.

"Yeah," agreed Karen.

"So… they're probably not ordinary bad dreams, then?" said Jade.

"Probably," agreed Karen.

"So what are they?" asked Jade. "And what do they mean?"

"I've got a friend studying psychology," suggested Karen. "Maybe we…"

"No," Jade interrupted. "No thanks."

"What about…" started Karen.

"I'm OK, really," Jade cut in. "I never wanted to see the counsellor in the first place."

"But…"

"Look," said Jade, interrupting again. "I've always known there's something more to these dreams. And now I'm sure." She suddenly looked determined. "And I think I know who I should be talking to about them."

✿   ✿   ✿

Jade dreamt of the storm again that night ... and the boy. The storm was not as severe. The boy did not look as sad.

"To save the future, start with the present," said the boy. His voice was familiar. *"Each step is important, and each individual can make a difference."*

☼   ☼   ☼

Marc came and sat next to Jade at lunch the next day.

"Sorry about being grumpy yesterday," said Jade, as she began eating her lunch. "I haven't been sleeping well."

After they finished their apples, Marc automatically placed his core in Jade's lunch box. Jade looked up at him and he smiled.

"I've been having weird dreams," started Jade.

She told him all about the dreams, about the session with the school counsellor, and about her talk with her sister. Then they sat in silence for a few minutes, until Jade looked towards Marc expectantly.

"Wow!" exclaimed Marc, eyes wide.

"Is that all you've got to say?" asked Jade.

"Um…" Marc shrugged.

"Great!" said Jade. "I thought that you might … I dunno … have some idea … something to say … maybe…" Her voice trailed off and she looked away.

"What?" said Marc. "Have a neat solution for you? Be able to explain everything?" He shrugged again, wracking his brains for something more to say — something to make Jade feel better about having told him everything. "Maybe … maybe the dreams are messages."

Jade turned slowly to look at him. "Messages?"

"Yeah. Messages from … aliens or something."

Jade began to turn away again.

"No! Not aliens. Maybe ... the dreams are messages from the future?"

Jade looked interested.

"Maybe things have gotten so bad with the environment," he continued, "that these future-people are desperate to get people in the past – that'd be us – to change their ways ... to start caring more for the environment ... and ... change the future ... make it better..."

"And they're doing this with dreams?" Jade raised an eyebrow.

"Well, maybe that's the only way of getting messages to the past." Marc was on a roll now. "First they tried your sister, but she didn't listen. And now they're trying you." He grinned at her. "You could be the chosen one. The one destined to save the world."

Jade looked back sceptically.

Suddenly they both burst into laughter.

"Dreams ... from the future," laughed Jade.

"To change the world," laughed Marc.

"As if!" they both hollered together.

As their laughter petered out, they both looked around at the school grounds they were in.

On the next bench, they saw someone eating a banana. A teacher walked along the path eating an apple. A young kid dropped a half-eaten sandwich into a bin.

"It's a pity the school doesn't have a compost bin," sighed Jade.

"Well," said Marc. "There's no reason why it shouldn't."

"Yeah," agreed Jade, thoughts of starting a school compost heap running through her mind. "You're absolutely right."

✿　✿　✿

There were no storms in Jade's dreams that night. The sun was shining and a pleasantly cool breeze blew across the water. The boy was standing on the golden sand as the water gently lapped at his feet. He was smiling.

"Thank you," he said. "The future isn't certain. So many things can happen. But you've given it a chance."

His familiar eyes sparkled.

"Thanks ... Great-Gran."

Jade woke up smiling ... and wondering.

Wasters

by Linda Newbery

My story began with the idea that people who live fifty years or so into the future will look back at the way we live now, and be horrified by how wasteful and extravagant we've been with the world's resources. Future generations will surely be wiser.

When Great-Grandad was a boy, people my age were called 'teenagers'. He'd been one himself.

I searched for it in my wordbank.

teenager noun; English (obsolete) a person aged between thirteen and nineteen years. Originated in the USA; in use in Standard English from about 1960 until the mid-21st century.

Great-Grandad said that being a 'teenager' meant not being a child but not being an adult either. 'Teenagers' had these few years when everyone expected them to be difficult, moody and selfish. It sounded weird to me – wasting that important time, when you were at your fittest for community work, and just coming into breeding condition.

"Hey, we're *teenagers!*" I said to Fern, trying out the word to see how it fitted. Only just: my thirteenth birthday had been three weeks ago.

"What's Standard English?" Fern asked, looking over my shoulder.

That's the trouble with research; you find out one thing and end up baffled about something else. But she answered her own question, as she often did. "Perhaps people were only allowed to speak English words. But that would be pointless. No one would understand you apart from other English speakers."

"That's another thing Great-Grandad said," I told her. "At school, they had to learn all these other dead languages – French and stuff. He didn't even *start* speaking Global till he was seventy-something."

"Anyway," Fern said, "what about *teenagers?* We'd better include them."

"Yeah. Put it down as a heading. We'll go and see Great-Grandad tonight, shall we? I want to ask him about Houses."

Fern and I were determined to win this year's Community Prize. The announcement would be made at a kind of graduation ceremony.

Everyone our age, in the last year of General Instruction, worked on their own project before passing on to specialised training. Next year I'd be in the Germination Unit, and Fern would follow her mother into Forestry. But we were planning to win that prize first. It was unusual for a boy and a girl to work together, but that made us all the more determined. Fern, being a girl, was in the fast stream for Instruction, and most of those girls either jeered at boys or ignored them completely. But Fern and I had been friends since our crèche days.

My great-grandad (really he's my great-*great*-grandad, but that's a bit of a mouthful) was a big help. There were lots of citizens who'd passed their hundredth birthday, but not many with such good memories. And memories were what we needed. We wanted our entry to be special. There were lots of presentations on tidal barriers or soil improvement, but ours, we felt, was a bit more ambitious. A bit more *intellectual*, and that appealed to Fern.

Tomorrow's community trip to Millennium Dome 2 would give us ideas. We'd seen the satellite pictures of the opening ceremony a month ago, with the President making a speech about the rebuilding of London. The new building was spectacular: a geodetic dome made entirely of glittering glass panels that caught the sunlight like the facets of a diamond. It was completely transparent, so you could see the lifts going up and down in the middle, like mercury in an old-fashioned thermometer. And we were actually *going* there, all the way to London. To be honest, I felt nervous about going so far from home, but our Community had been chosen as one of the first to send an Educational Group. I wasn't going to miss the chance just because I might be Transport-Sick. I'd heard that a lot of people were, their first time.

As soon as Fieldwork had finished, Fern and I took off our overalls and visors, and went to find Great-Grandad in the Senior Citizens' area. Some of the younger seniors were coming back from work, hand-weeding or banana-packing; they gathered in groups to drink herbal tea and watch the big screen or play games. Great-Grandad was sitting alone by the long window, with a book on his lap. Not many of the old folk read books, but I hardly ever saw Great-Grandad without one. A screen was no use to him.

"Hello, Great-Grandad," I said loudly, so as not to make him jump.

He turned round. His skin was lined with grooves like pine bark, grooves that became even deeper as his face creased into a smile. "Hello, Rowan-love! Have you got Fern with you?" He sounded pleased, but weary. He'd never really seemed happy since he retired, three years ago. He'd have gone on working if he'd been allowed to. I can remember him saying, "I'm no use to anyone! On the scrap-heap, at a hundred and one."

I had to ask, "What's a scrap-heap?"

That had made him laugh, and snap out

of his dark mood. "Of course, you wouldn't know, Rowan-love. We don't have scrap-heaps, now that we recycle everything. It used to mean a heap of rubbish."

But I'd had to look that up, too.

rubbish *noun; English (obsolete)* waste matter; something worthless

I still didn't get it. Nothing was worthless; it was the rule we lived by. It was a matter of finding the right use for things, and storing them till then.

Fern and I pulled up chairs next to him. Great-Grandad could remember all sorts of things; there'd been a *queen* when he was a boy, before England became a People's Republic, and he remembered some of the leaders we'd learned about in World History. Back then, England had its own leaders, and so did all the other countries. It wasn't surprising that all those different leaders made trouble, before there was a World Government. There had been wars – people had even *killed* each other. And all those leaders hadn't been able to prevent the Catastrophe.

"Can you tell us about Houses, Great-Grandad?" I prompted. Fern clicked her Voicechip to record his answer.

"Ah, Houses. Well, Rowan-love, we had Houses until well into this century. There were whole rows, whole towns of them – a House was for just one family, or sometimes for two people or even just one."

Of course, Fern and I knew that much – we all did – but it was unbelievable that Great-Grandad was one of the people who'd actually lived like that.

"And every single one of those Houses," he went on, "had its own heating, and its own lighting – no, I'm not exaggerating – and its own refrigerator and its own water-taps."

"But didn't anyone *realise*?" Fern burst in.

Great-Grandad shook his head. "No, not really, not back then. No one thought it was odd. We *all* lived that way. We took it for granted. And most people had a Car – you've heard of those, haven't you? A Car was like a very small Transport. You'd walk along a road and see hundreds of them. There were Cars parked outside most Houses. Some families even had more than one."

"Solar-powered?" I said.

Great-Grandad shook his head. "No. They ran on petrol."

"*Petrol!* But it's –"

"Yes, I know, love. Outrageous. Back then, you could just *buy* the stuff, from pumps by the roadside. As much as you wanted. And there were so many Cars that sometimes you could hardly *move*. I remember many a time, in my mum and dad's day, sitting in a Car in a long queue, going nowhere."

"Well, what was the point of that?" Fern asked.

"You may well wonder, Fern-love. But you see, people used to travel about, back then. That's why the roads were so busy. They'd live in one place and work in another. Some people even travelled from here to London and back *every day.*"

"What, in petrol-fuelled Cars? Just think of the – "

"I know, Rowan. But it was a different world, pre-Catastrophe. You'll see for yourself at the museum tomorrow. I only wish I could." Great-Grandad's eyes had gone misty; he was looking back into himself, at the world of eighty or ninety years ago. "We never thought, back then, that we'd be able to nurse the planet back as far as we have today. Never thought we'd able to grow crops again the way we do, and trees. Seemed like we'd all starve, or frizzle up. Yes, we've done well – thanks to people like your mum." He nodded in my direction. "And yours," he added to Fern.

"I'm going to work in Forestry, too,"

Fern told him.

"Good for you, lass. That's where the future is," Great-Grandad said. Then he turned towards the window. "Those birds out there – rollers, and hoopoes, and bee-eaters – they make a fine old din some mornings, but you can't beat a nightingale or a song thrush. I'd give anything to hear a nightingale again. Or a skylark, the way they used to burble in the sky. They're part of summer. *Old* summer, I mean."

I glanced out of the window at the birds flitting around the yuccas, oleanders and palm trees. A striped hoopoe was sitting on a canna lily to preen itself – pink bird against bright orange flower. Those nightingales and larks and thrushes Great-Grandad liked were just plain brown birds – I'd seen pictures. The ones we had now were far more colourful. But I said nothing, noticing that Great-Grandad suddenly looked very tired. Fern repeated the bird-names into her Voicechip; then I said, "We'd better go now, Great-Grandad. Thanks. We'll come tomorrow and tell you about London."

I looked back from the door. Great-Grandad was getting back into his book, his bony, gnarled-twig fingers running expertly over the Braille letters.

✿   ✿   ✿

On the Transport, I forgot to be worried about feeling sick; there was so much to see. We passed an ox-breeding unit, a coconut farm and two other Communities like ours, with citizens tending the crops – grapevines, soya and rice.

"On your left," our Instructor pointed out, "is land farmed by the Watford Community. You see the special cooled domes used for growing wheat, barley and potatoes. Of course they're still at the experimental stage, but I wouldn't be surprised if we could grow potatoes ourselves before too long."

Soon we were in the outskirts of London, and could see sunlight glimmering on water ahead of us: the London Basin. It was a busy thoroughfare for all kinds of shipping, with floating residences fringing the edges. We could see right across to Kent, miles away. Our Instructor reminded us of the drowned buildings under the water: ancient places like Buckingham Palace and the Houses of Parliament, and newer ones like the National Theatre and the first Millennium Dome.

"But why did they build the Millennium Dome in a place that was bound to be flooded when the polar ice melted?" Fern asked me.

I shrugged. "How would I know? It's hard to tell how their minds worked."

Our Transport circled the Inner Ring to Hampstead Heath, and there it was, ahead of us, glittering in the sunlight like an enormous diamond. Millennium Dome 2. The Transport went down a ramp that led right under the Dome, and a short lift-ride took us into the vast, airy atrium. We stood there under the tinted glass, blinking in the strong filtered light.

"Don't leave the building, and be back at this Collection Point by sixteen thirty," our Instructor told us.

There wasn't time to see everything, so Fern and I concentrated on what we needed most for our project. We headed for the tunnel that led to the early twenty-first century, emerging into a dark, eerie room lit only by the screens and displays.

We walked cautiously, even fearfully, as if we might get contaminated. Then I stopped dead and pointed. "Fern! Oh, yuk!"

"What – oh, that's disgusting! Were they *mad?*"

We were looking at a set of images from old magazines. To us, a magazine was a satellite programme, but these seemed to be large, soft books made of glossy paper. The one that had stopped me in my tracks showed a pale-skinned woman lying on sand. She wore hardly any clothes, just brief blue underwear. Her skin – repulsively pale and bare – made me think of the soft white slugs you find when you turn over a decaying log. But the really gruesome thing was that you could see the sun in the picture, shining down on her, and she was turning her face up to it like a tropical flower – smiling, as if she was *enjoying* it.

I shuddered. "Uurgh, that white skin! How did people survive? And what's she *doing?* Is it some sort of religious sacrifice?"

"No, silly! They used to do that on purpose. They liked it." Fern pointed to the lettering on the magazine: *Our Guide to Sunbathing.* It was written in English, but she knew enough to translate.

"*Sunbathing!* Another weird word." I entered it into my wordbank, and the answer came up.

sunbathing *noun, or participle of the verb* to sunbathe; *English (obsolete)* the act of exposing one's body to the warmth of the sun

So it *did* sound like a sacrifice!

"Puh!" I went. "Did she *want* to end up with skin cancer, or blind like Great-Grandad?"

"They didn't know, did they?" said Fern. "It wasn't really their fault. They were just ignorant."

There were *so many* things they didn't know, Back Then. The displays and interactive screens left me dazed and horrified. The twenty-first century was a desperate, savage one. I took in images of wars, famines, burning rainforests, shrivelling crops. And some of the things Great-Grandad had told us about: Rubbish Tips, and queues of Cars.

We were glad to get away, back to the clean air of our own time.

✧ ✧ ✧

When we visited Great-Grandad later that evening, he had a soggy parcel to give Fern. "Here," he told her. "I'm entrusting you with something precious." He put it into her hands.

She lifted the damp cloth. "What is it?"

"Bluebell bulbs," said Great-Grandad.

"Bluebells?"

"There are very few of them left now, so treat them carefully. You're going into Forestry – maybe you can save them from extinction. You've seen pictures?"

Yes, we thought we had.

"When I was a boy, there used to be woods full of them," Great-Grandad said, looking somewhere into the distance, as if he could see them now. "Whole drifts of them under the trees, in May, like cool blue water. The *smell* of them aah!" He breathed in, then sighed. "But we were too stupid to know what we'd got. We cut down the trees and dug up the earth and didn't realise what we were losing. What you must do," he told Fern, "is put those bulbs back in cool storage till you're ready to grow them. Cool, damp conditions, that's what they want. It's too warm for them to grow outside, these days. But you're the girl to do it. Trees," he added. "Those are the things. Trees to keep the air cool."

Fern looked doubtfully at the saggy bundle in her hands. "Well, I don't know if I can. What if it doesn't work?"

"But you'll try for me, won't you?" pleaded Great-Grandad. "I'd like to think that when I'm gone, there'll still be bluebells."

I saw Fern make up her mind. "Yes. Yes, I will," she promised.

✿ ✿ ✿

For the next fortnight, we worked hard on our presentation. I just knew we'd win. Ours was so brilliant that the judges hardly needed to bother with the other entries.

Everyone in the Community assembled in the Central Hall. The whole of the platform and gallery was taken up with displays. Fern and I sat with the other young folk at the front of the auditorium, and I fidgeted through all the presentations until at last it was our turn.

"*Wasters,* by Fern Glade and Rowan Fen," my own voice said, booming into the darkness, and then it began: our look back at the last century. All the citizens sat in silence, watching image after image of life Back Then. Grassland being ploughed up. A Road, hazy with Car fumes. Revoltingly, there were people eating chunks of dead animal. We'd shown a House, with someone tipping *rubbish* into a *dustbin* – Fern's voiceover explained what these old words meant. Then a picture of Earth seen from Mars, and Fern's voice saying, "They didn't mean to, but they almost killed the planet. Everything we do now is to compensate for the damage done by the Wasters."

"We've won. We must have!" I said into Fern's ear – almost shouting, or she wouldn't have heard for the applause that crackled into the air. I glanced at the audience, where I could see my mother sitting in a row with her father and my three grandads: Grandad, Great and Great-Great. I could tell by their faces that they all thought we'd won, too.

Ours was the last presentation, so now came an interlude for judging, with food served by the Community Catering Unit. It was a pity that I was too nervous to bite anything other than my nails. I was sure we'd be called up to receive the prize, though; so confident that I did something I never thought I'd dare. "Fern?" I said quietly. "When you're eighteen, do you think you might choose me as your breeding partner?" And I felt myself going red, because boys don't usually ask girls; they wait to be picked.

Fern looked startled, but seemed to give it

serious thought. "If you get genetic clearance, I'll consider you."

"We're a winning combination!" I told her. "We're about to prove that."

At last everyone came back to their seats for the prize-giving. The Community governor stood up to introduce the judge, Citizen Whitrow, a very old, white-haired man of about Great-Grandad's age. Citizen Whitrow got shakily to his feet, supporting himself with a stick. Then he held up his handscreen to read out the results.

"Third prize goes to Abraham Bud and Joseph Whitebeam for their collection of seaweed recipes." Applause. "Second prize is awarded to Sarah Baobab and Ruth Apfelbaum for their work on solar-cooled propagation units." More clapping, and a few cheers. I glanced at Fern, hardly daring to breathe; I saw Great-Grandad with his ears tuned for our names, and his hands held ready to clap energetically when our victory was announced.

"And now, citizens of the Community," Citizen Whitrow went on, with nerve-shattering slowness. "It gives me very great pleasure – very great pleasure indeed – to award first prize to – to... " Here he lost his place, fumbling with the handscreen. Fern nudged my foot with hers.

"...to Bullrush Greensward and Coriander Goldheart for their underwater topographic study of the London basin."

Applause and cheering crashed into my head and made my eyes sting. I couldn't look at Fern. When my eyes stopped blurring, I looked up to see Bullrush and Coriander being presented with their carved Oak Tree trophy. Then all the important Citizens on the platform crowded round to congratulate them.

I couldn't believe it. Not even a mention for *Wasters*! Nothing! After all that work!

Fern was tougher than me. She joined in the clapping, wearing a *that's life* expression.

"We got it wrong, Rowan, that's all," she said to me. "If I'd known who was judging –"

"What d'you mean?" I asked, thinking she meant it had been fixed.

"He wasn't going to choose *Wasters,* was he?" she said. "Guilty conscience. He's so old that *he* must have lived in a House, and driven a Car that ran on Petrol. I bet he threw away Rubbish. He was one of them, wasn't he? A Waster. He probably doesn't like being reminded."

"But that's not *fair!*" I protested. "All that effort – "

Fern shrugged. "At least we *did* it, and everyone saw. Anyway, we've got a new project now."

I wasn't sure I had the energy after today's defeat, but Fern obviously had. She looked across at the audience, where Great-Grandad sat looking sad and bewildered.

"The twentieth century wasn't *all* bad," she said. "You know those bulbs? If we get to work on a sealed, climatically-controlled dome, we can try to recreate a bluebell wood."

"All right," I said grumpily.

But she had a point. I thought of Great-Grandad's face when he talked about that sea of bluebells, and their cool scent.

We'd have a go at getting them back: for him, for everyone. We'd try to bring back something beautiful from the twenty-first century – that dangerous, short-sighted, narrow-minded Waste Age.

OK, Fern was right. It wasn't *all* bad.

But I wouldn't want to live there.

Now meet the authors...

Candy Gourlay wrote *How to Build the Perfect Sandcastle*

Candy had many amazing adventures as a journalist in the Philippines. To make ends meet, she took photographs, drew cartoons and dubbed movies with a fake American accent. Apart from the fake American accent, she has used all these skills to become a web designer in England where she now lives. Her amazing adventures inspired her to write books for children. Her novel *Tall Story* was nominated for the Carnegie Medal and shortlisted for the Blue Peter and Waterstones prizes.

Sea Canaries was written by **Susan Sandercock**

Susan lives near the River Thames in Essex,

England, and overlooks fields and marshland whilst eating breakfast. She'll often be seen walking in this location, which inspires her writing, and always takes her binoculars. Last year Susan sold her car to minimise her carbon footprint, which has given her extra money to spend on eco-friendly mini breaks by train. Susan loves cats, reading and all things pink and sparkly.

Francis McCrickard wrote *As Busy As...*

Francis was born in Cumbria, has lived in Africa and now works with young people at a retreat centre in Ilkley, West Yorkshire. He is married with three children. He has written books for teachers; a novel and short stories for children, and programmes for radio and television. At the retreat centre, he encourages young people to be more aware of how the way we live is affecting our climate and, with them, has planted nearly five thousand trees and a wildflower meadow.

Tommo and the Bike Train was written by **Miriam Halahmy**

Miriam writes fiction and poetry for children, young people and adults. Although she is a Londoner, her parents lived by the sea for twenty years, so her stories are often set by the sea, as well as in the Inner City. When she is not writing, Miriam loves to travel. She collects oceans – by paddling in them – and has four so far. Her ambition is to sleep out on the Antarctic ice and her favourite book is *The Secret Garden*.

Climate [Short] Change was written by **Lily Hyde**

Lily is from Britain, but has lived in and travelled around Eastern Europe and the former Soviet Union for over ten years. She's seen many climate changes in that time – in the weather, the economy, in society and families – and she writes about how they affect the places and people she's met. Her novels *Riding Icarus* and *Dream Land* are published by Walker Books.

Karen Ball wrote *Moonlight*

Karen was born and raised in Derbyshire, England. As a child, she spent many weekends walking in the Peak District with her family. She writes children's fiction, and her books have been about many different subjects including school plays, Pompeii and even samurai warriors. She writes in her spare bedroom, at a desk overlooking her back garden. Foxes, cats and magpies are often responsible for distracting her from her work. You can see details of her books at www.karen-ball.com.

Future Dreaming was written by **George Ivanoff**

George is an author and stay-at-home dad residing in Melbourne, Australia. He shares a house with two cats, two daughters and one wife. They have a 22,000-litre rainwater tank buried in their backyard, which waters their garden and flushes their toilets. George has written over 30 books for children and teenagers, and there are more on the way. Check out George's website at: www.georgeivanoff.com.au

Linda Newbery wrote *Wasters*

Linda Newbery has written more than thirty books for children and young adults, ranging from *Posy*, a picture book, to *Set in Stone*, winner of the Costa Children's Book prize, which was published for both teenagers and adults. She lives in a village in Northamptonshire, surrounded by trees and lush green countryside which she hopes will stay green and lush forever. Linda loves animals, so she doesn't eat them.

GIVE ME SHELTER
Edited by Tony Bradman

Sabine is escaping a civil war...
Danny doesn't want to be soldier...
What has happened to Samir's family?

Here is a collection of stories about children from
all over the world who must leave their homes and
families behind to seek a new life in a strange land.
Many are escaping war or persecution. All must
become asylum seekers in the free lands of the West.
If they do not escape, they will not survive.

These stories, some written by asylum seekers
and people who work closely with them, tell the
story of our humanity and the fight for the most
basic of our rights – to live. It is a testimony
to all the people in need of shelter and those
from safer countries who act with sympathy
and understanding.

REMEMBERING GREEN
Lesley Beake

It is the year 2200. Global warming has covered
most of the Earth in sea. The Tekkies, secure on
their fortified island, survive on dwindling resources,
but they need fresh water – rain. A sacrifice is needed,
something wild. But one African girl with her
lion cub, Saa, still carries the old knowledge
and is determined to thwart the Tekkies.

LINES IN THE SAND
New Writing on War and Peace
Edited by Mary Hoffman and Rhiannon Lassiter

Talented writers and illustrators from all over
the world have come together to produce this book.
They were inspired by their feelings about the conflict
in Iraq, though the wars covered in this collection
range from a 13th-century Crusade through the earlier
wars of the 20th century to recent conflicts in Nigeria,
the Falklands, Kosovo and South Africa, right up
to what was happening in Iraq in 2003.

With over one hundred and fifty poems, stories
and pictures about war and peace, *Lines in the Sand*
offers hope for the future.

All profits and royalties to UNICEF

FALCON'S FURY
Andrew Fusek Peters and Polly Peters
Illustrated by Naomi Tipping

Hidden treasure ... a secret crime ... the precious eggs
of a bird of prey... When Jan and Marie discover
who is stealing and selling the eggs of a peregrine falcon,
they suddenly find themselves in danger. Only the
ancient legend of Stokey Castle can help them –
and the falcon will show them the way.

Andrew Fusek Peters' and Polly Peters' exciting
new novel revisits the Klecheks, a family from the
Czech Republic newly settled in Shropshire.
Teenage brother and sister Jan and Marie are
soon unravelling villainy and mysteries,
but they will need even greater courage and
ingenuity to face what is about to happen.

ANGEL BOY
Bernard Ashley

When Leonard Boameh sneaks away from home
to do some sightseeing, little does he know that
his day out is about to turn sinister. Outside
Elmina Castle, the old fort and slave prison,
groups of street kids are pestering the tourists,
and before Leonard knows it, he is trapped
in a living nightmare.

Set in Ghana, this chilling chase adventure
is one you'll never forget.

CHRISTOPHE'S STORY
Nicki Cornwell
Illustrated by Karin Littlewood

Christophe has a story inside him – and this
story wants to be told. But with a new country,
a new school and a new language to cope with,
Christophe can't find the right words. He wants
to tell the whole school about why he had to leave
Rwanda, why he has a bullet wound on his
waist and what happened to his baby brother,
but has he got the courage to be a storyteller?
Christophe must find a way to break through
all these barriers, so he can share his story
with everyone.

FIRST GIRL
Gloria Whelan

When a second daughter is born to Chu Ju's family,
they decide that the baby must be sent away.
Chinese law dictates that a family may have
only two children, and tradition dictates that one
of them must be a boy. Chu Ju knows that she
could never allow her baby sister to go,
so she sets out in the middle of the night on a
remarkable journey to find a home of her own.

JOURNEY OF DREAMS
Marge Pellegrino

Helicopters slash through the air like machetes,
soldiers patrol the roads hunting down guerrillas ...
for the peaceful highlanders of Guatemala,
life has become a nightmare. Tomasa's mother
has to go into hiding with her eldest son, and,
when they see their house razed to the ground
and the villagers massacred, Tomasa, Manuelito
and baby Maria set off with Papa on a perilous
journey north to find Mama and Carlos. This is
Tomasa's story of how her family survives the
Guatemalan army's 'scorched earth' campaign,
and how their love, loyalty to each other and
Papa's storytelling keep them going on their
harrowing search for refuge in the United States.